DICING UP DISASTER

LITTLE DOG DINER, BOOK 6

EMMIE LYN

For all the rescue dogs and cats who have made my life richer in so many ways.
To my best friends ever.

ABOUT THIS BOOK

*A*nother day, another murder. At least that's what it's beginning to feel like in the small coastal town of Misty Harbor.

Who'd have ever guessed that owning the Little Dog Diner would put me right in the middle of deadly plot after deadly plot? No sooner had I put the last big mystery to bed, then another shows up at the diner's doorstep—literally.

Soaking wet and shaking with fright, this peculiar stranger tells me she and her enormous Newfoundland companion leapt overboard to escape a killer. Helping her stay safe will put me directly in the line of fire, but it's also the right thing to do. Can my Jack Russell terrier, Pip, and I save our two newest visitors from the already rolling wheels of fate *and* manage to keep the diner afloat?

We've never failed before, but then again we've never quite faced a case like this...

AUTHOR'S NOTE

Hi cozy readers!

Welcome to Misty Harbor on Blueberry Bay on the coast of Maine where cozy mysteries abound. Follow the continuing adventures of Dani Mackenzie and her spirited Jack Russell Terrier, Pip, along with many other great characters. Sit back and enjoy, but beware... murder is always on the menu!

Click here to sign up for my newsletter and never miss a new release.

1

*M*y stomach flipped as Luke and I approached the helicopter.

And not from enthusiasm.

"Won't this be amazing, Dani?" Luke's excitement about our scenic tour of Blueberry Bay on the coast of Maine should have been contagious.

Nope. Butterflies flapped helplessly in my stomach as I dragged my feet across the tarmac.

"I've always dreamed about doing this," he added.

Luke grabbed my hand and squeezed. Usually, a sure sign of affection but at the moment? As I tried to swallow my fear of heights, it felt more like a vice grip pulling me to certain death.

Okay, that's an exaggeration. This man who I,

Dani Mackenzie, expected to share my life with, and loved with all my heart, would do anything to make me happy.

Why hadn't I told him about my phobia when he'd surprised me with this six-month wedding anniversary gift? Truthfully, I didn't want to hurt Luke's feelings, but when he announced his plan, I sort of stuck my head in the sand thinking it wouldn't be too bad.

Now? My stomach lurched with each step closer. All I could do was hope I could contain my nerves and pretend to enjoy the flight.

Ace Osborne, Luke's friend, owner, and sole pilot of Air Adventures in Pine Falls, held his arms out in a big welcome.

"So glad to see you both," he bellowed enthusiastically. He gave Luke a hearty clap on the back and corralled me in a bear-like embrace. His big, burly frame dwarfed me.

"Are you excited, Dani? Luke's been champing at the bit for this day to arrive and," he waved his hand over our heads, "he couldn't have asked for a brighter blue sky. There's a bit of wind, though, so it might be a little bit choppy during our tour."

Great. I forced a smile as the butterflies danced faster.

Ace laughed and helped me into the helicopter. "That will just make it all the more memorable."

Would he call it memorable when I was holding my head over a paper bag?

I gulped down a bit of rising bile and smiled at both Ace and Luke. At the same time, I hoped my face wasn't looking too green. I silently scolded myself. *You got yourself into this mess, Dani, deal with it.*

Ace handed me a headset and buckled my seat belt properly before, Pip, my adventurous Jack Russell terrier, jumped on with me.

"Hold her tight so she doesn't fall off your lap, Dani."

I nodded, wondering who'd be holding me tight when this whirly bird dropped like a stone into Blueberry Bay.

Pip yipped. Her feet tapped happily on my legs, always excited for an adventure. With her ocean-blue bandana covered in tiny helicopters tied around her neck, a last-minute gift from my grandma Rose, Pip gave my chin a lick. I think she sensed my fear. In true Pip style, she was saying, *Chill out and enjoy yourself like I planned to do.*

"Easy for you to say," I told Pip. But I promised to try.

Luke looked at me with raised eyebrows. I pointed to Pip as if to say, we're in our Pip-to-Dani communication mode. Need I say more?

Ace started up the helicopter and ran through all the preflight preparations. I can do this, I told myself over and over as the rotors above us roared into action and gained speed. He looked over his shoulder and gave us a thumbs up sign.

As I stroked Pip, I felt the butterflies in my stomach settle a bit. Luke touched my arm and pointed out the window. The ground disappeared as we began to rise. The helicopter's smooth movement surprised me. No scary, breathtaking swoops like I'd expected. My stomach came along for the ride, unlike what happens sometimes when an elevator takes off too fast and my innards get left in the lobby.

I smiled, turning my head completely so I could enjoy the gorgeous view below. Yes, I *could* do this after all.

Amazing? Exhilaration swamped my dread when I realized that maybe this fear of heights had only been a figment of my imagination.

Blueberry Bay shimmered under the sun's reflections. Boats bobbed on the waves like toys in a bathtub, and Misty Harbor sparkled in all its sunny glory.

I comfortably settled in for our half-hour ride and glanced down at one boat in particular. It sped out of the bay, breaking the speed limit as it passed the area where many boats were moored.

Ace turned the helicopter to follow the curve of the bay, and I glimpsed activity on another boat. A big, black dog leaped off of a drifting cabin cruiser with a woman following close behind, leaving what looked like someone lying awkwardly on the deck of the boat. What was *that* all about? The ocean off the coast of Maine was never particularly warm, but in June, it was absolutely too frigid for a swim.

Familiar warning tingles lit up my nerves.

I strained my neck, desperate to keep the swimmer and her dog in view, hoping they made it safely back on board after their cold dip. Instead, with a strong stroke through the waves, the woman swam away from the boat toward Misty Harbor right behind the dog. I hit Luke's arm to get his attention and jabbed my finger toward the swimmers below us. He leaned as far as possible toward my side, but we'd flown out of view.

Luke shrugged his shoulders, pointed to his ears, and shook his head. Apparently, with the helicopter racket drowning out my words, he had no idea what I'd been trying to tell him.

What could I do up here above Blueberry Bay?

At least I'd forgotten all about my fear of heights.

But that didn't help as a new fear for the safety of the woman and dog took its place. What could it possibly mean?

I tried to focus on the beautiful scenery as we flew over Blueberry Bay and the surrounding towns, but I was itching to land and find out what had happened to the mystery duo. And the person still on the boat.

Pip whined and scratched at the window. I think she sensed the same unease I had.

Finally, Ace turned the helicopter back toward the small airstrip, and it was all I could do to keep my legs from bouncing Pip right off my lap.

At last, with my feet firmly planted on solid ground, I told Luke and Ace about what I'd seen.

Luke arched his brow. With a tilt of his head, he said, "You do have an overactive imagination, Dani."

Ace laughed. "Nothing wrong with that."

But without giving a second thought to my information, he asked, "Are you two heading to the Little Dog Diner now? I have a craving for one of your famous lobster rolls, Dani."

This was the first of four days off for us. Luke had carefully planned to fill our extra-long weekend with surprises, including a picnic for the two of us after the helicopter ride. Now, though, how could we say no to Ace after he'd treated us to this scenic tour? Plus, it would give me a chance to call Detective AJ Crenshaw and let him know about what I'd seen.

Just in case there really was a problem.

Our picnic would have to wait.

2

I left Luke and Ace sitting at a booth in the Little Dog Diner, loudly discussing the helicopter ride.

With a promise to take care of their lobster roll request before I called AJ, I walked into the kitchen. My two employees, Chad and Christy, had the midday rush completely under control.

"Three lobster rolls, please," I said to Chad.

"Oh, Dani." Christy looked up and wiped her hands on her apron. "You surprised me. We weren't expecting you to stop by today, but it's good you did." She grabbed my arm and pulled me toward my small office, stopping just outside the closed door.

In a low voice, she whispered, "Someone is here, and she refuses to leave until she talks to you."

"Who is it?" I couldn't imagine who would be looking for me here on my day off.

Christy shrugged. "She wouldn't say, but she's stubborn, soaked, and your office smells like the ocean seeped in with her."

That certainly piqued my curiosity. I opened the door, letting Pip scoot in first, but she stopped short when a black dog, the size of a miniature horse, lowered its enormous head to sniff my ten-pound white terrier.

I backed up a step or two.

This was beyond weird. A big black dog, a person who more closely resembled a drowned rat than a young woman, and the distinct odor of seaweed now in my office? It had to be the pair I'd seen jump overboard, but why had they ended up here?

"Danielle Mackenzie?" the woman asked as soon as she saw me.

"That's right," I answered cautiously. "Who are you?"

The woman, dripping water across the floor, pushed the door behind me, closing it with a loud click. "I'm Sunny Shaw. You don't know me, but I need your help."

"I saw you jump off a boat," I told her.

Her mouth fell open. "How? Who else saw me?" Panic fueled her questions.

"Listen," I said, opening a small closet behind my desk. I pulled out dry clothes I always kept there in case of a bad spill that soaked right through my apron. I sized her up and pulled out a pair of gym shorts, a t-shirt, and a sweatshirt. "We're close enough to the same size. Take these into the bathroom and get out of those wet clothes. You're chattering louder than a woodpecker hammering on an old dead tree." I grabbed a couple of towels, too, handing the clothes and one towel to Sunny. "I'll dry off your dog in the meantime. What's his name?"

"*Her* name. Jasper." Sunny clutched the bundle of dry clothes to her chest and disappeared into the bathroom.

"Okay, Jasper. How about a nice rub down?" I let her sniff my hand, waiting for a friendly tail wag before I draped the towel over her back and rubbed.

By now, Pip had regained her composure after her initial surprise. With her front legs down, and her behind in the air, her tail wagged enthusiastically.

I knew what she had on her mind. "Let me dry

your new friend off first, Pipster. Besides, it's too small in here for the two of you to start romping around." With the size of Jasper dwarfing Pip, any playtime needed to move outside.

Pip looked at me. To get her crazies out, she chased her own tail. Jasper watched with her tongue hanging out one side of her mouth, but fortunately, she didn't copy Pip's antics, or she would have turned my office upside down after one circle.

Sunny returned holding her dripping pile of clothes. She must have found a comb in the bathroom because instead of the wet straggly mess it had been, she'd styled her hair into a neat French braid exposing a purple streak winding in and out of the dark braid.

What struck me the most, though, were her eyes. I'd never seen such a bright blue with a hint of purple. Startling and almost too intense to be real.

She cleared her throat and dumped the soggy pile on an empty chair. "Thank you," she said, her voice barely a whisper. Jasper moved to Sunny's side and leaned against her leg. "You said you saw me jump off the boat?"

That wasn't important. I wanted to hear her story, but first we needed to address the mystery of why she was here and how she knew who I was. "How about I get us something to eat and then we can talk."

Sunny nodded but didn't move.

"Would you be more comfortable eating in here?"

She nodded again.

"Sit down and I'll be right back." I left her in the office with the two dogs while I made a beeline into the diner. Wait until Luke hears this, I thought. Now maybe he'll take me seriously when I see something suspicious.

I slipped into the booth next to Luke, interrupting his deep discussion with Ace over their lunch choices. They put down their menus, apparently anticipating dessert, and I described my unexpected guests. Luke said, "You're joking. Why?" which, of course, was the question of the hour.

"I haven't gotten that information yet. She's hungry, so I'm getting us something to eat, and then I'll try to get her to spit out her story. She came here looking for me, Luke. She said she needs my help. Something is very strange about this picture."

Ace, following my conversation, said, "You know, I saw a boat race out of Blueberry Bay. A cigarette boat, which is built for speed. Do you think it could be connected?"

"What do you mean?" I'd seen that boat, too.

"Dani, there's a lot of strange stuff that happens on the water. Why would a young woman jump overboard, swim to shore, and show up here when you don't even know her?"

"I have no idea."

"Exactly. That's why the two incidents might be a coincidence or more likely they're connected. That's only my opinion, mind you."

Christy arrived at the booth with rolls over-flowing with fresh pink lobster meat and crispy golden fries on the side. My mouth watered. I picked up one of the plates and got to my feet. "I'll need one more and I'm eating in my office," I said to Christy.

"No problem. I'll bring it in as soon as it's ready."

Luke reached for my arm just as I was about to walk away. "It's nice of you to feed this woman, Dani, but this is your day off. Send her on her way when she's done. Don't waste all day with her."

"I hope it's that simple, Luke. You and Ace enjoy your lunch, and I'll let you know what's going on as soon as I can."

As I walked away, I heard Luke tell Ace that I had a knack for getting involved in every mystery in

Misty Harbor and, how, along with Pip, I'd helped solve several murders. I knew he worried about me, but I could also hear pride in his voice. I hoped this wasn't the beginning of another one of those issues that sucked me in whether I liked it or not.

I opened my office door.

Sunny's eyes went straight to the platter in my hands. I handed it to her. "I'll wait for the next one. Go ahead and dig in." I dug out a couple of dog treats from my desk, offering one to Jasper first, sitting politely, and then to Pip.

My guest hesitated for several seconds before she sat down and rested the plate on her legs. "Are you sure?"

I appreciated how courteous she was, but at the same time I imagined threads of drool hanging from her lip.

"Yes, of course. Help yourself." I sat on my desk chair wondering when any of this would make sense. "Pull up to my desk and use it for a table before all that deliciousness ends up on the floor. Although Pip wouldn't mind cleaning up a food mess."

Sunny grinned at Pip. "That's your name? Fits you perfectly." She raised her head and looked at me. "She's well-behaved and shared her space with

Jasper without complaining." She started in on the lobster roll with such intensity, I decided to give her a breather from any questions until she'd filled her stomach.

There was a tap on the door, and when I said, "Come in," Christy appeared. "I've got your other platter. Want me to bring it in?"

I walked to the door and took the tray from her. She'd added two glasses of iced tea, too. "Perfect. Thanks." I didn't give her a signal, but I think she picked up that I wanted time alone with my guest.

She glanced around me to get a peek at Sunny but didn't say anything. No doubt Chad had asked her to get some information about the stranger in our midst, but I didn't know much more than they did at this point. As difficult as it was, I wanted to tell her to practice some patience, but all I could do was thank her and close the door.

As soon as I sat down again, Sunny set her half-eaten lobster roll on her plate. "Benny told me to find you if anything happened to him."

"Excuse me?" I blurted out.

"You know, if he got hurt or something," she said. As if *that* explained anything.

"Who's Benny?" I said as I picked up my lobster

roll. I tried to act as casual as possible, so I nibbled on my lobster roll.

Sunny's face sagged and tears filled her eyes. "Benny was my friend. It was his boat I escaped from."

Was her friend? Why the past tense? And escaped from? What the heck had I witnessed?

3

*S*unny snuffled and swiped the back of her hand across her eyes, her lobster roll forgotten on my desk.

"Benny planned to show me the coastline around Blueberry Bay today on his boat, Fish Tales. He was hired to study the environmental impact of developing a piece of property in Pineville. The property is owned by his friend, Hunter Bodane, who owns the Nine Pine Nursery. He wants to sell but Benny believes the shoreline should remain undeveloped."

I nodded, encouraging her to continue. I listened to her tale while I ate fries and sipped my iced tea.

"And then, that horrible guy came onto Benny's boat."

I coughed into my glass. "What guy?" Was she talking about the boat speeding out of Blueberry Bay around the same time I'd seen Sunny jump overboard? This was all too confusing. And now scary.

"I don't know," she said, her voice beginning to crack. "That's the problem. I'd gone into the cabin to use the bathroom and heard a motorboat roar up beside us. Then I felt a jolt. I thought someone had rammed right into Fish Tales. Jasper went berserk, barking like a maniac. She attacked the cabin door trying to get out."

"You must have been terrified," I said, remembering when I'd been trapped in a boat by someone intent on killing me.

"To tell you the truth, I was so scared, I froze. Right there, sitting in that teeny tiny bathroom rectangle with my pants down. I couldn't have moved if my life depended on it, which it probably did. But I think Jasper's uproar kept whoever came on board away from me." Sunny hugged the huge head resting in her lap.

Pip, never one to be left out, especially if someone was in need of some extra love, squeezed herself onto Sunny's lap and licked her chin.

"They left?"

"Yeah. I heard the boat roar away just like it had arrived. I waited for what felt like hours before I moved off that spot. In reality, it was probably only a few minutes. You know how time stops when you're so scared you can hardly breathe?"

I nodded. I knew exactly what she meant.

Sunny took another bite of her lobster roll before she continued. "I waited, and waited, hoping Benny would find me and tell me what the heck had happened."

I sipped my drink but never took my eyes off of Sunny's face. "He didn't come down to see if you were okay?"

She shook her head as her eyes filled with tears again. "I finally crept out of the bathroom. It was quiet. Too quiet. Only the splashing of waves against the hull was louder than my own breathing at that point. I peeked out the door and that's when I saw him."

"Benny?"

She nodded. "He was lying on his back. Blood splattered everywhere—the deck, chair cushions, a green jacket." Her voice dropped to a whisper. "They murdered him."

With a jolt, I remembered seeing someone lying awkwardly on the deck of the boat when Sunny and

Jasper jumped overboard. Horrific. "Who was on that speeding boat?" I asked uselessly. I knew Sunny didn't have an answer.

"The killer," she said. "That's all I know for sure."

"I'm so sorry, Sunny. Have you called the police yet?"

"No. I came straight here. That's what Benny told me to do. He said you'd help me. I don't know anyone here in Misty Harbor."

I wracked my brain trying to think if I knew a Benny but came up blank. "Why did he think I could help?"

"He didn't say but I had no idea what else to do. I didn't know how to drive his boat, so I jumped overboard and swam with Jasper. I'm a strong swimmer, but I think it was all the adrenaline that helped me get to shore. That and Jasper. She stayed right with me. I hung onto her and let her tow me when I was too cold to continue. Honestly? I was ready to give up and let the ocean end my nightmare."

I looked at Sunny and Jasper sitting there, bonded together with the strength of steel. Like Pip and me. "I have to ask, Sunny. Why did Benny think something might happen to him?"

"All he told me was that he was doing this study to protect Blueberry Bay. I guess he knew he might ruffle some feathers since not everyone cares as much as he does... did... about the shoreline. But... murder?"

I had to agree. Murder was a final solution. Benny ruffled a lot more than a few feathers.

"I'll be right back," I said. "I have to step outside." As soon as I was out of hearing distance of the office, I called Detective Crenshaw. I gave him the bare bones of Sunny's story. Then I said, "You need to come to the diner about the murder."

"You said murder?" AJ spoke so loudly I had to hold the phone away from my ear.

"Calm down." I yelled right back at him. And then, in case my voice carried into the office, I spoke softly so I wouldn't upset Sunny more than her already frazzled nerves indicated.

"The murder didn't happen here at the diner, AJ. This is where you can talk to Sunny Shaw and get the details from her. And, send someone out to check on a boat on the bay called Fish Tales. That's where you'll find the victim."

"How do you always end up in the middle of this stuff, Dani?" AJ's voice was quieter, but his tone was still hard as nails.

"Like I can control this?" I asked. I heard my tone rise in frustration. "Just get over here, okay?"

"On my way," he said before the call went dead.

I stepped back into the office and Sunny jumped. I think she had her ear to the door.

"Is this guy gonna bite my head off?" she asked. "I came here to find you and ask for your help, not have you sic an angry detective on me." She stood up and headed toward the office door. "I'm going home. Just tell him what I told you."

"Wait a minute, Sunny. I totally understand how you're feeling right now—scared and alone."

She stopped with her back to me. I could see her shoulders shaking. I'd guessed correctly. Sunny Shaw needed a friend right now more than anything. I couldn't let her walk out to fend for herself in this town where she knew no one.

I guided her back to the chair and knelt in front of her. She hung her head, refusing to look at me even when I pushed a few stray hairs from her face. "If you run away, it will look like you've got something to hide. Trust me about this. It's better to face the police now. I'll stay with you."

Her tear-streaked face finally lifted to meet my gaze. My heart about cracked with grief for this frightened young woman.

She nodded just as Detectives Crenshaw and Winter walked into my small office space.

I squeezed Sunny's shoulder, hoping it conveyed some strength. Her fingers twisted in Jasper's soft fur, and Pip, always fearless and loyal, stayed close.

"Hello, Detectives. This is Sunny Shaw."

With Sunny leaning against me, I had to worry about where this would lead, dragging me along whether I wanted to or not.

4

*D*etective AJ Crenshaw rested against my desk, arms and legs crossed, a posture that implied intimidation more than welcome to town.

He and I had known each other since we were kids. Our friendship was complicated at best. Sometimes it worked fine because of our mutual friend, Maggie Marshall, but when we got involved in police investigations, we butted heads. Maggie had a private investigation business and she had her own ideas about hunting down bad guys. Let's say when the three of us got wind of a case, it could get complicated.

I worried how Sunny would hold up.

AJ's partner, Detective Jane Winter, who'd moved

to Misty Harbor a little over six months ago, wore her professional mask. It could mean anything from sympathy to *I don't believe one word coming out of your mouth.*

I hadn't expected both detectives to descend on Sunny. This double-barrel assault spelled big trouble.

"Ms. Shaw?" AJ said in his gruff, all business mode.

"You can call me Sunny," she answered in a stronger voice than I'd expected. Good for her for trying to bring a level of friendliness to the conversation.

"Sunny then," he said. "How about you tell us your story." Jane leaned against the door frame, listening intently.

No questions? I had a sneaky suspicion that they'd already discovered Benny's body on Fish Tales and wanted to match her side of the story to the facts they'd uncovered. I wished I'd told Sunny to be totally honest before they'd arrived. Had I thrown her to the lions?

Sunny glanced at me.

I nodded and gave her an encouraging smile.

She picked up her glass of iced tea from my desk and took a long drink. After draining the glass, she told Detectives Crenshaw and Winter what she'd already told me.

"This boat you say rammed Fish Tales," AJ said. "Did you actually see it?"

"No. I was in the cabin bathroom, but I heard a loud motor and felt something ram into Benny's boat. Whoever killed him had to come across the water, right?"

"That's what we'll have to determine." Jane tipped her head and narrowed her eyes before she continued. "What I can't understand is, why did you come here to the Little Dog Diner? Are you and Ms. Mackenzie friends?"

Sunny shook her head. "I told you already that Benny told me to come here. That Dani would help me."

Okay, that wasn't going to ingratiate me toward AJ or Jane. I saw them both share a glance and frown at each other, confirming my suspicion.

"How exactly do you think Ms. Mackenzie can help you?" Jane asked. "Does she know who was driving the boat you suspect ran into Fish Tales?"

Again, Sunny shook her head, but she also sat up a little straighter. "I don't know how she'll help me going forward, but she already gave me dry clothes and food. That's a start from someone I've never met before. I guess you could say she's a kind and compassionate person."

I was really starting to like Sunny Shaw. She was gaining confidence against these two tough detectives and she gave me one of the nicest compliments I'd received in a long time. Who wouldn't enjoy that?

"Those clothes don't belong to you?" AJ asked. "Where are your things?"

Sunny pointed to the soggy pile of clothes she'd stripped off.

"We'll have to take them." Jane pulled on gloves and took a plastic bag out of a small duffle I hadn't noticed before.

Sunny lurched out of the chair. "Why are you taking my stuff?" She sounded frantic.

Jane ignored her and pushed the wet pile into her bag, then handed a paper to Sunny. "Sign this so you can get your belongings back."

"What's going on? You think *I* killed Benny?"

"Please sit down, Ms. Shaw. This is just routine," Jane explained. "As far as we know, you were the only person, other than the victim, on Fish Tales. We have to collect any possible evidence that will help us solve this crime."

Just routine? I knew better. Of course, they suspected Sunny and unless they found this mystery boat, she'd probably be charged with murdering her friend.

AJ hadn't moved from the edge of my desk and still stood with his arms folded. "Dani, didn't you and Luke take a scenic helicopter ride over Blueberry Bay this morning?" he asked, though he knew the answer to his question.

"We did." My stomach clenched. Where was he going with this?

"I talked to Luke and the pilot on our way in here. Luke told me that you saw Sunny jump overboard. Why didn't you call right away to report that?"

I gulped and scrambled for an answer, looking from Sunny's worried expression to Jane, who seemed ready to pounce.

"Once we landed, that was my plan until I got here and found Sunny waiting in my office. She was soaked, cold, and hungry. As soon as I handled that, I did call you, or don't you remember?" I glared at him, knowing it wouldn't win me any points, but I was firmly on Sunny's side and had to stand up to AJ before he ran over both of us.

"You didn't think to call us *immediately* when you saw that body on board?"

"I didn't know there was a *body*. I saw someone

lying on the boat. Could have been someone sunbathing for all I knew. I had no idea when we flew over in the helicopter that the guy was dead. We only had the boat in view for a very short time."

"But you did see Sunny jump overboard."

"Yes. First Jasper jumped then Sunny."

"And that didn't strike you as odd? The Atlantic Ocean at this time of year is only forty-five to fifty degrees." His dark eyes bored right through me like he suspected I might be hiding something.

"That's exactly why I gave Sunny a change of clothes and food when I found her here. She needed to warm up as quickly as possible." Of course, I thought it was odd, but I didn't need to confirm AJ's question. He'd made his point.

He turned his attention back to Sunny. "That's what I can't figure out, Ms. Shaw. How did you manage to swim from Fish Tales to shore in that cold water? Most people wouldn't have made it."

"Well, I'm a strong swimmer and when the cold started to affect me, I hung onto Jasper, and she towed me to shore. She's part Newfie. In case you didn't know, the Newfoundland breed is known for their water-rescue ability. If she hadn't been with me... you'd probably be searching for my body. That is, if anyone even missed me."

"If you'd stayed on the boat, you wouldn't have risked your life in that cold water. Wouldn't that have been the safer choice?" Jane asked.

"I never considered staying on the boat. Once I saw Benny dead, I panicked. I was afraid that whoever did that to him might very well decide to come back. I had no intention of waiting around for that."

I had to agree with Sunny's quick decision.

Jane picked up her duffle with Sunny's clothes and who knew what else inside. "Oh, one more question," she said as if this was the least important of all since she acted like it had almost slipped her mind. "Did you fix food while you were on the boat? Cut bread or fruit or anything like that?"

I sensed there was a lot behind this question, but Sunny just shrugged and shook her head. "No. Benny brought a basket of food, but we hadn't touched it yet."

"So, when you left the cabin, you saw Benny dead and immediately jumped overboard?"

"Well, I didn't stop to fix a sandwich if that's what you're asking." I could see how Sunny put Jane's questions together and came up with that snippy answer, but it didn't even make the corner of Jane's mouth twitch.

"No, I'm asking if you *did* anything before you jumped overboard."

Sunny paused, probably replaying the moment, which had to be difficult. Her eyes widened. She looked at me before she answered Jane in a barely audible voice. "I picked up a knife that was lying next to Benny but dropped it before I followed Jasper overboard."

"Don't leave town, Ms. Shaw," Jane said, her tone final and cold.

This complicated everything.

5

"What do I do now?" Sunny asked me as soon as the two detectives left. "They think I killed Benny, don't they?" She paced in my small office with Jasper right next to her.

"I don't know what *they* think." I hated to ask but it had to be done. "*Did* you kill him?"

Sunny's mouth dropped open, then she clamped her jaw and snarled, "Is *that* what you think? The answer is *NO!*"

I touched her arm. "I'm not trying to upset you, but I needed to get that out of the way. Let's go." I held my hand out for Sunny to exit my office ahead of me. "I've got an idea for where you can stay until you're allowed to leave town."

She still didn't move. She stood her ground

blinking and shaking her head. "I can't figure you out. First you throw me to those two detectives to defend myself and then you ask me if I killed Benny, like you'd ask a customer in your diner if they'd like a cup of coffee. Now, you say you have a place for me to stay. Why should I trust you?"

"Whether you believe it or not, I *am* trying to help you. I didn't throw you to those detectives. You were at the scene of a murder. You didn't think they'd just let you waltz out of town without questioning you, did you? If you don't want my help, fine. What's it gonna be?" I stared at her with my hands on my hips, sort of hoping she'd walk out so I could rid myself of this mess.

With her hand on Jasper's head, Sunny still didn't budge. "What about Jasper?" Her voice faltered. "I won't go anywhere without her."

"Don't worry about Jasper. I know someone who'll welcome her with pats and treats. Come on then, it's just a short walk. Fresh air will do us both good. It's time to look forward instead of backward and get you out of this dilemma." I had to shake this horror even if Sunny couldn't. "My best friend recently bought one of the oldest inns in Misty Harbor, the Blue Moon Inn. She'd be happy to offer you a room in exchange for some work. What do you think?"

I didn't actually know if Lily would agree with what I'd just said. It was a big imposition. All I could do was ply Lily with my best puppy dog eyes and promise her whatever she wanted to make this happen.

Sunny let out a big sigh as if her whole world was shattered, and she had nothing to lose at this point. "Okay." She grabbed the rest of the lobster roll and took a bite. "Thanks for the food. It's amazing."

I put my arm around Sunny's shoulder, guiding her, Jasper, and Pip out of the diner. "Wait here and finish your lunch. I'll be right back. Oh, and you should probably let someone know where you are."

"I already did," she said.

I left Pip with them, as proof that I really was coming back, and went in to find Luke. He and Ace had to be wondering what had taken me so long.

The diner, filled with all the typical noises that were a comfort to my ears—happy chattering, silverware clinking on plates and bowls, and the deep fryer sizzling in the kitchen—helped to settle my nerves.

"Hello stranger," Luke said with a hint of frustration in his voice. "I thought you'd found something better to do today than hang out with me."

I slid in next to him and rested my head on his shoulder. "Oh, you must mean hanging out with my brand-new friend who Detective Crenshaw thinks is a murderer? Yeah, that ranks right up on my list of favorite things to do."

"That bad?" he asked. He snaked his arm around my shoulder and pulled me close. "Did she do it?"

"I don't think so. But if it wasn't for that boat speeding out of the bay not long before she jumped overboard, I might have trouble believing her story. It all fits together like it's more than a coincidence."

"I saw that boat, too," Ace reminded me. "It was one of those high-powered boats built for speed—a cigarette boat—not a pleasure fishing cruiser." He slipped some money under his plate. "I have a charter flight to get to. Catch you guys another time. Good luck with that new friend, Dani." He winked at me and smiled a lopsided grin.

He must be quite the heartbreaker I thought as he scooted out of the booth.

"What's next?" Luke asked now that we were alone.

"Here's my plan. Sunny can't leave town so—"

"Please don't tell me that we have a new roommate."

Luke was more than tolerant about the arrangement at Sea Breeze. He accepted Pip as part of the family, of course, and Rose loved her new apartment, which Luke had added on to the main house before we said *I do*. I certainly didn't want to rock the boat.

"Nope. Here's my plan. I'm bringing her to the Blue Moon Inn. Now that Lily is working round the clock to get everything perfect for the grand reopening, I'm sure she can use some help. She has a group of people arriving tomorrow night before a brunch meeting on Saturday. Sunny can help in exchange for a room." I smiled, satisfied with my idea. "What do you think?"

"You're a genius. But I already knew that." He tucked money under his plate. "A tip for Christy, the rest is on your tab?"

"Clever, Luke." I bumped his shoulder as we walked out. "You're so lucky you married the owner of the Little Dog Diner. I hope your lobster cravings don't put me out of business."

"Hey. I trade blueberries for everything I eat here. Did you forget that?"

"Hmmm. Blueberries for lobster... you've got a point."

Luke held the door open for me, "Hope you don't mind if I tag along with you. This is our day together, after all, and I don't dare let you out of my sight or you might pick up a few more strays—either the two-legged or four-legged variety. You don't seem to discriminate."

I jabbed him with my elbow. "If I were you, I'd worry more about the four-legged variety. As a matter of fact, I rescued one of each today. Wait till you see Sunny's dog, Jasper. She probably counts as two of the four-legged strays." I nodded my head to the side of the diner. "See?"

"Is that Pip sitting underneath that giant?"

I had to laugh at my little Pipsqueak sitting in front of Jasper's two front legs. Her head barely reached the big dog's chest.

Luke whispered, "Jasper could pull Pip in a cart. I've still got one in my barn. Wouldn't that be cute?"

"We'll see. Sunny?" I waved to get her attention. "Meet my husband, Luke Spencer.

Sunny didn't smile. Instead, she looked up and down the street, and I thought for a moment she might bolt.

Jasper stood up, wagging her tail with a friendly hello. That was a start.

What had I gotten myself into?

6

"**R**eady?" I asked Sunny, ignoring her silence.

Pip did her happy dance around my legs, letting me know *she* was ready for fun regardless of what anyone else was going to do. Jasper, too, acted eager to get moving.

Sunny groaned as if she held the weight of the whole world on her shoulders. I cut her some slack. I put myself in her shoes, all alone and reeling from the murder of a friend, afraid the killer was after her now.

"I guess I don't have much of a choice, do I? I don't have any other options but to go with you." Her snippy tone almost made me tell her I had better things to do, but I decided on a pep talk instead.

"That's one way to look at it." I waited until I was sure I had her undivided attention. "Or you could adjust your attitude and work on figuring out what exactly happened this morning on Fish Tales. When you decide to quit feeling sorry for yourself, maybe you'll remember some important details that Benny mentioned." I tilted my head and felt one eyebrow jump, leaving Sunny with this challenge to take charge of herself.

A darkness filled her eyes. "I won't deny that I'm struggling now, but I say this with complete confidence: I never quit."

That's exactly what I wanted to hear.

"I want to go to my house and get a few things." She held her arms out to the side. "My own clothes for starters. And," now her expressive eyes took on a glint of mischief. "Benny left a folder at my house this morning. That's a good place to start looking for answers. Could you give me a ride?"

I looped my arm through hers, deciding I liked this Sunny Shaw person after all. With her newfound attitude, I knew I could work with her. "I'll see what I can do but let's get you settled at the Blue Moon Inn first. If I can explain to Detective Crenshaw that you have a place to stay in town, he might be more inclined to let you go to your apartment." And if he insisted that Sunny stay in Misty Harbor, he couldn't keep me from getting her stuff.

Sunny nodded. With a determined pep in her step that I hadn't seen before, she followed Pip toward the Blue Moon Inn.

At the black iron gate that led to the inn's front door, Sunny hesitated. "This looks way fancier than what Jasper and I are used to. Are you sure we can stay here?"

The Blue Moon Inn, one of the oldest establishments in town, recently changed hands with my best friend Lily at the helm now. She'd never been happier, putting her creative talents to work in the kitchen and hosting intimate events in the beautiful, renovated space.

I knew I'd have to play to Lily's sympathetic side, but yes, I was confident that she'd come around to my idea. The secret was that I didn't plan to give her a chance to say no.

"Trust me, she'll love to have some extra help," I said.

Luke reached for the door and ushered us in first. I almost swooned at the aroma of Lily's trademark cinnamon rolls welcoming us into the foyer.

Her favorite classical flute music softly played in the background.

"Lily?" I called as I led the way through the house to the spacious light-filled kitchen.

Racks of cooling deliciousness covered the spacious island workspace from edge to edge.

After Lily wiped her hands on her apron, she brushed her hair out of her face. A smudge of flour on her cheek took the place of makeup these days. "To what do I owe this pleasure?" She eyed Sunny before giving me her what's up expression.

After introductions, Lily ushered us into her comfortable all-purpose sitting room. "Dani, can you help me get refreshments for everyone?"

Lily knew me too well. She certainly must have guessed that my arrival with a stranger meant I had something up my sleeve. I was in the hot seat now, owing her an explanation before dumping Sunny in her lap. "Be right back," I said to Luke and Sunny, before following my friend.

Lily turned and stared at me as soon as the door closed behind us. "Who have you dragged in now?" she asked. The frustration in her voice masked her usual friendly tone.

"I'm up to here with work." She held her hand several inches above the top of her head. "You know

I have to get ready to host an important meeting that will kick off my grand opening."

"And that's exactly why I'm here." I put the kettle on and grabbed her big wooden tray. It was easier to keep busy while I spun my tale. "Do you need help for a few days?"

"Why?"

I put cups, sugar, cream, and the hot water on the tray. "Here's the thing." I leaned against the counter and plastered on my most endearing smile. "Sunny needs a place to stay for a few days. She could help you in exchange for a room. Great idea, right? You just said you've got a ton of work on your plate."

"You mean Sunny, who just walked in here five minutes ago, who I know nothing about? That big dog belongs to her? And, most importantly, the part you've left out: why does she need a place to stay?" Lily narrowed her eyes and fixed me with a stare.

This was more difficult than I'd expected. It must be a reflection of the level of stress Lily felt with this first big event right around the corner. Or, possibly, the fact that she's known me forever and well, I do have a tendency to stumble into the middle of problems. Some bigger than others and this one looked to be a whopper. "I guess the town grapevine hasn't done a good job yet."

"What happened? And please don't sugar coat it, Dani."

"Fair enough. Here's the thing, Lil. Sunny Shaw showed up at the diner needing help. She and her friend, Benny Chadman—"

"Wait. Stop. Right. There. Benny Chadman? He's supposed to be the featured speaker at the meeting."

Uh oh. This was bad. "Not anymore, Lil."

Her jaw dropped. "What do you mean?"

"Like I was saying, Sunny and Benny were out on his boat and someone murdered him. She jumped overboard and found me." Not a speck of sugar coating added, just like Lily wanted.

"That's horrible. Why did she find *you*?"

I shook my head. "Benny told her to find me if anything happened to him. I never met either one of them before today."

Lily slumped onto one of her kitchen chairs. "I can't believe this."

"Not to sound heartless, but maybe the meeting will happen anyway. I mean, it's all paid for, right?"

"I suppose."

"So, can Sunny stay here? AJ told her she can't leave town."

"That means she's a suspect! If word gets around about her, how will I explain *that* to my guests?"

Yeah, I hadn't thought about that little detail. "Let's take it a day at a time. See how it goes. Okay?"

"I *could* use some help."

I forced myself not to look pleased that Lily appeared to be softening, slightly. At least, until she had time to digest everything.

"All right. She can stay tonight but I can't promise any longer than that. We'll see how it goes."

"And her dog?"

"He's awfully big."

"But very sweet," I quickly said.

"You know I can't say no to you, Dani, but you'll owe me a lot for this favor. How about you make the clam chowder for the meeting? I'm planning a pear, blue cheese, greens salad with a raspberry vinaigrette followed by a cup of soup before the main course. If you make the chowder that will be a big help."

"Done. Anything else?"

Lily's eyes held a glint of something I couldn't define, but I was sure it had a lot to do with me. "I'll think of something." Her lips twitched at the corners and I knew we were okay. Okay in the sense of Sunny staying at the Blue Moon Inn and Lily was still talking to me. As for what she had in mind for me repaying this favor, I'd have to wait and see on that.

Now, my work was cut out for me.

With a deadline.

Yikes!

7

*W*hile Lily gave Sunny a tour of the inn, Luke and I took the two dogs for a walk. It was the least I could do while she showed Sunny around.

Jasper, Sunny's big, goofy, lovable dog, might be a problem when guests arrived for Lily's brunch meeting. How I'd manage that, I didn't know yet but there it was, a mess I had to solve one way or another.

"Uh-oh," Luke said. I looked up and saw AJ striding toward us with a no-nonsense gait. From the stern look in his eyes, he wasn't here for a friendly, how are you guys doing chat.

I waved and smiled like he was just the person I was hoping to see. In a way, that was true. "AJ. I have an update about Sunny for you."

He stopped and waited for me to continue.

If AJ intended to intimidate me, he succeeded, but only for a moment. I stammered a bit then spit out. "Lily agreed to let her stay at the Blue Moon Inn."

"Good to know," AJ said behind his professional mask. "I'm sure I'll have more questions for her after the Pineville police finish searching the victim's house."

More questions? Why hadn't I figured that into my plan? AJ would never allow Sunny to leave Misty Harbor, even for a change of clothes. I'd have to take care of that myself.

I did a quick calculation. With a half-hour driving time each way and another half-hour to pack up what clothes she needed and anything else she wanted, we should have more than enough time. Two hours tops. In and out. Hopefully, before the police decided to search her place, too, if it came to that.

"You promise me that Sunny will be at the Blue Moon Inn if I go looking for her?" AJ asked.

"Really, AJ? I can't promise that. I'm not planning to chain her to Lily's stove or anything like that. All I can give you is my word that she agreed to stay at the inn. Are you suggesting that she can't even go outside to take her dog for a walk?" I patted Jasper's big head. "You asked her to stay in town, and she agreed to that. She's not exactly under house arrest since you haven't charged her with a crime."

AJ sucked in a big lungful of air. Maybe he was trying to bite his tongue after my snitty remark. "All I'm saying, Danielle, is please don't get up to anything funny."

I was ready to give him a piece of my mind, but he held up his finger.

"Wait a minute for crying out loud. Let me finish." His exasperation was evident. I'd almost pushed him over the edge. "I know how you get yourself involved in these dangerous situations, Dani, and I don't like it."

"AJ. I'm only trying to help this poor, lonely frightened young woman."

"Good," he said. His expression didn't match his words. "I hope that's all you're trying to do because I think she could be in danger."

My jaw dropped at that statement. I'd been thinking all along that AJ was about to arrest Sunny Shaw for murdering her friend, Benny. I never saw *this* angle coming at me. "What kind of danger?" I asked, though I wasn't sure if I wanted to hear the answer.

"Serious danger, Dani. I can't define it any better than that. If what she said is true, that someone came on board to murder her friend, that someone would see Sunny Shaw as a loose end that needs tidying up. Understand?"

With that, AJ fixed me with his steely gray eyes, leaving no doubt in my mind that there was a lot more to this mystery than what appeared on the surface.

A shiver ran up my spine. I pulled Jasper closer to me, trying to communicate the seriousness of the situation to her. She was Sunny's guard dog now. She'd protected her once already and very well might need to again.

Luke took my hand. "We hear you loud and clear, AJ. We'll keep our eyes on Sunny."

I loved the *we* in Luke's statement. I was so lucky to have him in my life.

"Good. Sunny shouldn't be out walking around by herself," AJ said. "Just a precaution."

AJ started to walk away but stopped and turned back to face us. "Dani?"

Oh no. He had something else to say that I wasn't going to like.

"Watch *your* back, too."

"What are you suggesting? You think *I'm* in some

kind of danger?"

AJ glanced up and down the street. I did too. Was he looking for a lurker out to get me?

He lowered his voice. "Here's the thing. Because of your helicopter ride this morning, if there was a boat that carried the killer to Fish Tales, that person could be worried you witnessed their crime. We aren't releasing that detail so tell Sunny to keep it to herself, too. I've already talked to," AJ scanned through his little notebook, "Ace from Air Adventures, to let me know about any unusual requests for a charter or anything else out of the ordinary."

I was speechless. Something new for me. I'd given my story to AJ and had nothing more to tell him. I could feel my nerves fraying; I've never liked being in danger or in the dark. Too bad I hadn't told Luke about my fear of heights. Instead of flying high in Ace's copter, we could have celebrated our sixth month anniversary with a quiet drive away from Blueberry Bay and missed out on all the drama.

Wishful thinking got me nowhere. Anyway, Sunny would have still been waiting for me at the diner when we returned. So, no matter how I looked at it, some force I didn't understand was intent on pulling me into this mystery.

"What should we be watching out for?" Luke asked. Good question.

AJ counted off his team's legwork. "We're looking into all of Benny's recent interactions, including his marketing business, personal contacts, or even chance encounters. Sunny should wrack her brain, too. In the meantime, don't panic, just be smart." He forced a smiled that came across as a hollow expression.

Finally alone on the sidewalk, Pip jumped on my leg, bringing me back to our original plan. Walk the dogs.

I could handle that.

But I carefully studied everyone we passed.

Who murdered Benny Chadman and why did he tell Sunny Shaw to find me if anything happened to him?

There had to be a connection, and I had to find it.

8

*M*y walk with Luke and the two dogs was not the relaxing or refreshing outing I'd hoped for, despite the blue sky overhead. AJ's stern warning left behind an unsettling feeling of gloom.

At least, when we returned to the Blue Moon Inn, Lily had Sunny working cleaning the windows. I explained our plan to pick up what she needed from her apartment.

"But I want to go with you," she complained.

"You can't just up and leave your window-washing job and risk losing your comfy accommodations here."

Sunny gave me a reluctant nod of her head, just as Jasper plopped down right next to her with a loud sigh of contentment. She was comfortable right where she was and didn't plan to get up anytime soon.

"I'll give you a list," Sunny said, caving in to my wishes and Jasper's contentment. "Along with my house key."

With her address in Luke's GPS, we set off in my dark green MG for Pineville, following the twisty-turny road that provided random glimpses of Blueberry Bay. Eventually, the directions turned us inland where leafy majestic maple trees shaded the roads.

"What do you think, Pip?" I asked as she perched on my legs taking in the passing scenery. Unfortunately, she couldn't tell me her inner thoughts. But, if I was a betting woman, I'd say she was hoping we'd stop and take her for a walk so she could sniff out chipmunks in the rock walls.

She yipped at the side of the road and Luke said, "Don't tease Pip like that, Dani."

Oops. That thought must have slipped out.

"You know how the words w-a-l-k and c-h-i-p-m-u-n-k are her two most favorite things. If we want to get Sunny's items and return to Misty Harbor quickly, we don't have time for a w-a-l-k right now."

He shook his head. "I can't believe I have to spell around your brilliant dog."

"Sorry," I said into the Pipster's ear. "That w-a-l-k will have to wait."

I scanned Sunny's list and chuckled at the specific descriptions she'd made.

"Listen to this, Luke."

I read from her note. "The first item is a blue t-shirt, in the top dresser drawer, at the bottom of the pile. If it's so special, why is it at the bottom?" I lowered the list onto my lap. "Really? If I brought a different one would she ask me to go back? Also, jeans hanging in her closet; her bathroom supplies packed in her travel bag hanging on a hook behind the bathroom door; Jasper's bed in the living room; Jasper's bowl, and food in the kitchen closet."

I read on silently until the end. "This last one—a manila folder tied with a string on her kitchen counter under the coffee maker. Okay."

She'd underlined that with a thick black line. I guess she thought it was important. "She told me the folder had Benny's notes and stuff that he'd left there, intending to pick up when he brought her home."

"What kind of information?" Luke asked, taking a quick glance from the road to look at me.

I shrugged, wondering how Luke thought I'd know that. "Sunny only said it had to do with his study of Blueberry Bay." I watched the landscape whiz by without really taking it in. "According to her, it has information from a study of Benny's concerning a development project and ideas to help a friend rebrand his business. Those two things might be connected, but I'm not sure."

"What kind of business?"

"I tapped my finger on my lips. "Something nursery. Maybe Nine—"

"Nine Pine Nursery?" Luke provided the rest of the name that had slipped my memory.

"Yeah. That's it. You know that place?" It sounded vaguely familiar, but I couldn't come up with any concrete specifics in my memory bank.

"We've been there. Maybe you don't remember. They have perennials, annuals, herbs, and even a greenhouse filled with flowers, plus lots of gardening type gifts. From what I've heard though, the owner, Hunter something or other, is having a big cash flow problem. It's a great piece of property. If I'm not mistaken, it does have a small border with Blueberry Bay."

"Maybe that's the connection," I said. "Benny was

trying to help his friend save his business, *and* he was studying the Blueberry Bay coastline."

The GPS interrupted our conversation to say we'd arrived at our destination—a small house at the edge of Pineville, both tidy and inviting. At least on the outside.

But something made my nerves tingle.

I paused before opening the MG's door. "Do you think that while Benny was studying the shoreline, he discovered something?"

Luke slid out of his side of the MG. "That's a logical assumption. We could ask Benny's friend if he knows anything. After we look to see what's in the folder Sunny asked us to pick up. With any luck, there will be something to point us in the right direction for answers... or more questions."

Now I couldn't wait to get inside. "Let's go, Pip."

Luke and I waited near Sunny's front door while my curious terrier poked her head under the bushes. I didn't mind waiting and checking out the street. For what, I wasn't sure, but if Sunny was in danger, this could be where the bad guys would look for her.

Nothing out of the ordinary caught Pip's attention or mine for that matter. Sunny's neighborhood seemed absolutely normal. A jogger passed by, and a neighbor across the street peeked out her window. I wiggled my fingers in her direction. Bell chimes from the local clock tower reminded me we'd used up half the afternoon already.

I chalked up the normalcy as a good thing.

But, as I reached to unlock the front door, it slid open a crack.

I gasped and grabbed Luke's arm. "Should we just leave?"

Around us, birds chirped in the quiet, sunny afternoon. A breeze ruffled my curls. Pip didn't have her ruff up so why did all my nerve endings scream: watch out!

Luke pushed the door with his finger. The hinges squeaked as it swung open about a foot more. "Maybe Sunny forgot to pull her door all the way closed when she left," he said.

"Maybe." That was one explanation. But I imagined someone waiting inside for her to return. Instead, they'd find us.

Pip dashed inside, tail wagging, and looked back at us as if to say, the coast is clear. What are you two waiting for?

Her enthusiasm gave me confidence to enter even while doubt swirled in the pit of my stomach.

Something just felt wrong.

9

*L*uke entered Sunny's gray shingled Cape Cod style house first. I stayed close behind scanning every corner, barely registering her furniture and belongings, as we moved deeper inside.

He stopped, turning to check on me and I crashed into his back.

"Really, Dani?" He swept his arm around Sunny's spotless apartment. "Nothing out of order. Pip is completely at home. What's got you so darned jumpy?"

Good question.

Before I could answer, a car door slammed. Foot-steps tapped up the walk outside.

"Pineville Police!" I heard someone call on the other side of the front door.

Pip charged. She meant business, not that the police would be impressed.

The front door slammed open, revealing a policeman with his weapon aimed right at us.

Adrenal surged through me.

My arms shot up in the air.

"I got a call," he said. "What are you people doing here?"

Pip backed up but didn't stop her warning growl. I guessed that my friendly wave to Sunny's neighbor when we'd arrived hadn't set her at ease. She'd probably called the police.

"We're getting a change of clothes for Sunny Shaw," I said. Should I explain more? "I'm Danielle Mackenzie and this," I nudged Luke with my raised arm, "is my husband, Luke Spencer." I was glad one of us could think clearly since Luke seemed stunned into silence. "And that's Pip" I said, to complete the introductions.

The cop holstered his gun. "What happened to Sunny and Jasper?"

"They checked into the Blue Moon Inn in Misty Harbor for a few days. She's not supposed to leave town."

He squinted his eyes. "Does this have anything to do with Benny Chadman?"

I nodded, wondering why he'd jumped to that conclusion. "You heard what happened?" By then, I figured I could lower my arms.

"Sure did," he said, checking out the dining room off to our left. "I came over here to make sure Sunny was okay after a neighbor called to say a couple of strangers walked into her house. She went boating with Benny today on Blueberry Bay."

I glanced at Luke, then said, "She's okay; Jasper is too." I picked up Pip to keep her from annoying the policeman. "Do you want me to ask her to call you or give her a message from you?"

"Yeah, that would be great. We're... good friends. Tell her to call Mick Walker. She's got my number." He closed the door behind him. "Want me to help you get her things?"

"That's not necessary." I held up Sunny's house key hoping he'd understand that she'd tasked us with that job. Better yet, I hoped he'd get the message to leave. "She explained what she wants us to get for her. We're just going to pack up and get going." I tried to make my voice light and friendly. I didn't want him to see the folder and start asking questions.

"Okay. Tell her I can come to the Blue Moon Inn if she wants me to. My shift is over at five. I figure she might want to talk about Benny since I knew him, too." He seemed to think that gave him some importance. Maybe it did and maybe it didn't.

"I'll let her know." I looked at Luke, leaning against the wall.

Mick stayed put. Was he planning to keep an eye on us until we were done? Finally, he opened the door. "Okay then," he said, and left.

"That was kind of weird," Luke said twisting around to look out the window. "He just believed everything you told him?"

I looked over Luke's shoulder but didn't see anything of interest on the street. "I bet he already ran a check on my license plate before he came inside. He probably already knew my name. I don't know. Let's get Sunny's stuff and get out of here. This place is giving me the creeps."

"I know what you mean," Luke said. "I didn't feel those weird vibes until he arrived."

I led the way, determined to find the kitchen. I checked the list as I walked. "Let's start with the last item—the folder. As far as I'm concerned, that's the most important." I looked around a doorway. "Here we are."

"I'll get Jasper's food and bowl. Isn't that in here somewhere, too?" Luke asked.

"Yeah, check the closet over there." I pointed to a door next to the refrigerator. I saw the coffee maker and slid it sideways over the granite counter. I reread the list. "That's weird."

"What?" Luke asked as he lugged a big bag of dog food out of the closet.

"The folder is supposed to be under the coffee maker." I lifted up the toaster and felt under the microwave in case Sunny hadn't remembered correctly. "Nothing."

That odd tingle crept back up my spine. "Do you think someone's already been here and stolen it? Luke? Do you think someone might still be here?"

"I don't know, Dani. Let's just go." He held up the dog food and a ceramic bowl. "I'll grab Jasper's bed on the way out."

"What about Sunny's clothes? We're here now. If someone's hiding upstairs, wouldn't it be better to flush them out and find out who it is?" I set Pip down. "She can go upstairs first. If a burglar's hiding, she'll find them."

Luke grabbed a cast iron skillet off the stove.

"Do you really think you'll need that?"

"I hope not, but I'd rather be safe than sorry. Let's go."

I pointed up the stairs and Pip shot to the top, fearless on top of cute and lovable. Luke and I watched her disappear around the corner but heard no yipping. A good sign. I tiptoed up a couple of steps with Luke right behind.

Pip reappeared and looked at us with her tail wagging. I knew this look and it meant: what are you waiting for? I let out a deep breath.

"I think it's safe upstairs," I said.

"Then why are you still whispering? Let me go first." Luke squeezed past me, and I didn't complain.

At the top I saw a bathroom flanked by two other doors, which I guessed were bedrooms on either end of the short hallway.

"I'll grab her bathroom stuff." I tried to sound confident, but this whole mission was eerie. "You'll wait here in the doorway?" I asked Luke.

He nodded, planted his feet, and crossed his arms with the skillet sticking out.

Of course, when I entered the small space, the first thing I saw was a closed shower curtain.

I trembled but took a deep breath, stepped forward and with one brave swipe, yanked it to one side.

Empty. I actually sagged with relief.

Luke laughed at my reaction. I snorted, sending both of us into fits of uncontrolled laughter. After that release of tension, I concluded that *if* anyone was hiding in Sunny's house, they'd flee to get away from the wackos on the premises.

"What did you expect to find in there, Dani?" Luke asked between more bouts of laughs.

I clutched Sunny's bathroom gear to my chest and tried to scowl at him. It didn't work when I replayed my actions because it sent me into another round of laughter. "I didn't know. That was the problem. But you could thank me for getting us both laughing in this crazy situation."

"True. Thanks." He put his arm around my shoulder. "Let's get the rest of Sunny's stuff and hope we don't find anyone lurking in her dresser drawer." I didn't miss the twitch at the edge of Luke's lips.

"Or under her bed," I said.

We followed Pip into what appeared to be Sunny's room based on the lived-in look of clothes draped over a chair and the unmade bed. I was glad to know I wasn't the only one who sometimes forgot to tidy up in the morning before leaving Sea Breeze.

"Grab some jeans out of her closet," I said to Luke as I pulled her dresser drawer open. I scooped up the whole pile of t-shirts, thinking she'd need more than the blue one. Something fell out from the bottom of the pile and clunked on the floor.

A beautiful gold necklace in the shape of a sun glittered at my feet.

This must have been why the blue t-shirt was so important to Sunny. I tucked it safely in my pocket and dropped the whole pile of shirts in a tote bag hanging behind the door. I added underwear and the jammies laying on her bed along with the jeans Luke found in her closet. Scanning her room, I picked up a pair of sneakers and tossed those in, too.

"Good to go?" he asked.

"I think so, but let's take another look in the kitchen in case we overlooked that folder."

We hurried back down the stairs and filed into the kitchen. I scanned every inch of countertop, the top of the fridge, and each chair seat. Nothing.

A white rectangle under the kitchen table caught my eye just as I was about to give up.

"What's that?" I pushed a chair out of the way and picked up a folded piece of paper.

"Probably some junk mail that slipped off the table," Luke said.

I unfolded the paper. "I don't think so. This is interesting." I looked at Luke. "It's a list of names under the heading Blueberry Bay Study with Police Officer Mick Walker's name first."

Luke looked over my shoulder at the list. "The second name is, Hunter Bodane, owner of Nine Pine Nursery."

"And Benny's friend," I said.

10

J tucked Sunny's belongings behind the seat of my MG, and Pip jumped on my lap. "Ready," I signaled, and Luke pulled away from Sunny's house.

As we passed her nosy neighbor's house, I caught the curtain flutter. Did that busybody know more than she realized?

Luke had his eye on the road but made a suggestion. "How about we drive by Nine Pine Nursery," he said. "I want to know why Hunter's name is on that list you found. Maybe his relationship with Benny is more complicated than we think."

"Good idea," I said but my heart wasn't in it. "I'll pick up some plants while we're there." Sure, I loved a good mystery, but not on the day I had planned to take off with my husband. "I reached over and rubbed Luke's neck. "Sorry this day isn't going the way you'd planned. Your poor picnic basket is still tucked in the back. Could I peek inside when we get to the nursery?"

Luke, always a good sport, rewarded me with a big smile. "I like how you think. A snack sounds perfect right about now."

After a few more turns on the country road, he pulled into a big parking lot at the Nine Pine Nursery. He parked near rows of colorful displays of potted plants and garden statues arranged in front of a glass greenhouse.

While I admired the plant selection, Luke dug into his basket and rewarded me with two chocolate covered strawberries. "What do you think about this?" he asked.

"Yum! Now, that's what I call a delicious surprise."

"Ready?" Luke asked after the strawberries had vanished.

"Yup."

Pip bounded out of the car as soon as I opened the door. She jumped into a wagon meant for customers to cart their purchases, sitting as pretty as a princess.

"Really?" I said to my prima donna. "You expect me to pull you around?"

"What a cutie," someone said behind me. "She'd make a great promo photo for my website."

I turned around. "Hunter Bodane? You're just the person we were hoping to find."

"Well, that's about the best thing I've heard all day. What can I do for you?" A lanky man, in his early thirties I guessed, looked at us and flashed a friendly smile. "Is it okay if I give your dog a treat? I keep a supply in my pocket for all four-legged visitors." He shoved his hand into his overall pocket.

"Only if you want to have a friend for life," I said. "Pip never forgets anyone who keeps a supply of treats around."

"Pip, huh. That fits you to a T." Hunter crouched in front of the Pipster and held his hand out with a small dog bone. She politely accepted the gift.

He straightened and asked, "Now that my favorite and most important task is taken care of, how can I help you two? Are you looking for anything special?"

"Actually," Luke said, "we're hoping you can tell us about your friend, Benny Chadman."

"Benny? What would you like to know except he's dead set against me selling all this?" Hunter swept his arm in an arc. "Benny's the type... don't take this the wrong way because I love Blueberry Bay, but you know, sometimes progress gets in the way of the status quo."

"What kind of progress?" I asked trying to sound curious and not skeptical.

"Well, it's not public yet. All I can tell you is that it does *not* involve any kind of condo development or strip mall. But that's not good enough for Benny. He wants me to either keep my business as is or sell the development rights to a conservation group. Don't get me wrong, it's a great idea, but that won't cover all my investments at this point. He doesn't understand that part of my reality."

Luke nodded. I knew he understood overhead and investments because he dealt with those issues for his farm, Blueberry Acres.

"So? Benny?" Hunter straightened a couple of pots that had tipped over. "Don't tell me that he's convinced you to buy me out for some environmental program. I wouldn't be surprised if he's trying to throw a monkey wrench into this other plan before it gets set into motion." He smiled but it didn't reach his eyes, which told me this issue he had with Benny went deep.

And, I assumed Hunter hadn't heard the news

yet. Everything he'd told us about Benny was present tense. "Benny's a good friend of yours?" I asked.

He flicked his wrist. "We go way back. Yeah, good friends but not close friends, if that makes sense. Benny and I aren't always on the same page about everything. One of his problems, in my opinion, is that he doesn't have to work for a living. He can pick his projects and live off his trust fund. So, he doesn't really understand the reality of my situation where work equals profit. Hopefully." He shrugged like it wasn't a big deal. "I guess you could say that we agreed to disagree about financial stuff. Why all the questions?" Hunter glanced at his phone and it looked like he replied to a message.

"Benny was murdered this morning," I told him.

His head shot up away from his focus on his phone. "What?"

"Benny is dead."

"That can't be. He took Sunny out on his boat this morning." Hunter's hand covered his mouth. "Is Sunny—"

"Sunny's okay," I interrupted, watching his reaction carefully. It seemed genuine, but here was another person who knew Benny's whereabouts. Despite saying they were friends, Hunter seemed to have a least one major disagreement with him.

"What happened?" Hunter had moved to one of the plant benches for support.

"I don't really know the details." This was mostly the truth, but it wasn't for me to share the little I did know. "Can you tell us anything about Officer Walker?"

"Mick? Is *he* involved? He wasn't a big fan of Benny's, that's for sure."

I touched Hunter's arm. "Oh, no, I have no reason to believe that he's involved, it's just that he showed up at Sunny's house while we were picking up some things for her. It seemed... odd."

"He is odd, and he has a thing for Sunny, if you get my drift. For some reason, she tolerates him, but she tries to keep her distance as much as possible. That's probably why Benny didn't like him much. He referred to Mick as Sunny's stalker."

That was an interesting piece of information. Especially if it was Officer Walker who took the folder that Sunny asked me to bring back. Of course, I had no proof he took it.

"Where is Sunny? You said you were picking up some things for her?"

I picked up a gallon pot of lavender and set it in the wagon next to Pip. A perfect thank you gift for Lily. "The police in Misty Harbor asked her to stay in town. So," I held up my hands. "Here we are."

"I didn't catch your name. Are you and Sunny friends?"

I had a feeling that Hunter was beginning to work backward through the information, desperate to figure out the bigger picture from the limited information I'd provided.

"Actually," I said, "I only met Sunny this morning. She came looking for me at the Little Dog Diner. I'm Dani Mackenzie, and this is my husband, Luke Spencer. We're just as confused about all this as you seem to be. For some reason, Benny told Sunny to find me if anything happened to him. He must have suspected that he was in some kind of danger. Did he ever mention anything to you about a concern?"

Hunter waved at a car driving into the parking lot. "Benny was always kind of paranoid. He had a history of suspecting someone was out to get him. I didn't really pay much attention to his theories."

"He was right this time," I said letting Hunter know I wasn't taking his comment lightly.

He moved away from us. "I have someone I need to help." A woman wearing high heels, a pink pencil skirt, and a white blouse walked toward Hunter. "Crystal. I just heard about Benny."

"Crystal?" I whispered to Luke. "There's a Crystal on that list, too. This is getting more curious with every person we talk to."

"And they're all connected to each other. Let's pay for your plant and get out of here, Dani. There's something going on that smells like a dead fish on a hot summer day. I'm afraid you're smack in the middle now."

I couldn't believe that a simple trip to pick up a few things for Sunny at her house in Pineville would turn up more questions than answers. I was afraid Luke was right. When Sunny Shaw showed up in my office, she pulled me right into the thick of this mess.

We had to go back and talk to her.

11

*L*uke carried the remaining chocolate-covered strawberries and Jasper's dog bed while I juggled the lavender plant and Sunny's bag into the Blue Moon Inn.

As soon as we walked inside, Jasper loped over. She was obviously thrilled to see Pip who danced on her back feet to reach the big dog's head for some mutual sniffing.

I dropped Sunny's bag near the door and headed toward the sound of voices trickling from the kitchen.

Every surface was covered with pots, pans, plates, and even every piece of Lily's silverware. "Mice," Lily said with her nose wrinkled in disgust.

"I'm not sure these cupboards have been cleaned out since this inn was built."

That had to be an exaggeration, but I certainly wasn't going to argue with her.

"No worries," Sunny said. "Everything you see here has been washed, dried, and I've just finished scrubbing all the cupboards and drawers. No harm done."

Lily took Sunny by her shoulders, moving her away from the cupboards. "You've gone over and above already. Now, go take a break with Dani and Luke."

"Are you sure, Lil?" I asked. "We could all help put everything away."

A quick flash of horror passed across Lily's face. "Absolutely sure. I know how I want everything organized, so I'll finish this job," she said. She did help herself to one of the strawberries from the box that Luke held out to her before she shooed us out of her kitchen.

I hated to see Lily looking so overwhelmed, but I completely understood her desire to work uninterrupted while she found a place for all of her kitchen equipment. What's worse than looking for a baking pan only to find a cupboard full of plates instead? I ushered Sunny into the inn's big sitting room and set my lavender plant in the window. With a sweep of my hand over the leaves, I released the calming odor into the room.

"Lily totally exaggerated the mouse problem," Sunny said, taking a seat with Jasper lying at her feet. "I found one cupboard in the coat room with mouse evidence, nothing in the kitchen, but Lily went crazy. She couldn't risk a guest complaining to the health department."

I studied Sunny. With her legs tucked under her body, nibbling on a chocolate covered strawberry, and one hand trailing over the arm of the chair patting Jasper's head, she presented an image of a relaxed and confident person. The wet, frightened woman I'd met in my office, a distant memory.

"We brought clothes from your house. And I found this." I handed her the gold necklace.

Tears filled Sunny's eyes as she fastened the beautiful piece of jewelry around her neck. "Benny gave it to me; said it represented my sunny personality. I gave him a gold pen because he was always jotting down notes to himself.

That must have triggered a memory because the next thing Sunny did was lean forward and plant her feet on the floor. "What about that folder in the kitchen?" Desperation filled her voice.

Whoa, that wasn't the reaction I'd expected. I glanced at Luke before I asked Sunny, "What was in that folder?"

She stood up and paced. "I don't know. You didn't look inside? Where is it?" Her eyes filled with worry as she stared at me. "This is bad," she mumbled to herself, seemingly lost in her own terrified world again.

Before I gathered my thoughts, the front door of the inn opened. Heavy footsteps approached.

"Sunny Shaw?" AJ's deep voice penetrated every corner of the sitting room. "Pineville's Officer Walker has some questions for you. I informed him that I'd bring you to our police station here in Misty Hollow. You need to come with me now."

She looked at me like somehow I'd be able to change this request. As calmly as I could, I said, "Tell Lily that Detective Crenshaw has called you down to the station and you'll be back as soon as possible."

Her eyes widened with that unmistakable look of fear she got every time anything about the murder came up. She nodded, though, and headed toward the kitchen.

AJ held his hands up before I had a chance to ask him a question about Officer Walker. "Listen, Dani. Before you get all up in my face trying to protect this

person who, don't forget, you really know nothing
about, I promise to stay with her. This murder is in
my jurisdiction, but I need Pineville's cooperation
depending on where the evidence leads us.
Understand?"

"But—"

"No buts, Dani. That question only has one
answer. Sunny Shaw is coming with me."

I glanced at Jasper waiting at the door for Sunny
to reappear. "What about her dog?"

AJ shook his head and rolled his eyes. "I know
you, Dani, and you always take care of any dog in
need. Maybe this time, with your hands full with
that great big dog, you won't have time to stick your
nose where it doesn't belong."

Maybe AJ couldn't do two things at once, but
apparently, he didn't know me as well as he
thought. Multi-tasking was my middle name. A dog
in need? That was all the motivation necessary to
solve the underlying problem. What he didn't know
was that Luke and I had already uncovered some
interesting information. With his current attitude, I
had no intention of sharing those tidbits. For all I
could imagine, he'd put me under some kind of
house arrest to keep me from asking any more
questions.

I smiled agreeably at AJ hoping he'd assume he'd won this discussion.

AJ looked at the door where Jasper still waited. "What's taking Sunny so long? Did Lily give her one more job to finish?" Irritation laced his words. He checked his watch again. "I'm going to find her. I don't want to keep Officer Walker waiting."

He pushed through the door, too quickly for Jasper to squeeze through with him. She whined, and her sad, brown eyes practically broke my heart.

"Let's take Jasper for a walk and see if that distracts her," I said to Luke.

As soon as I opened the door, the big dog pulled so hard on her leash, I almost fell flat on my face. "What's got you all in a hurry?"

"Pssst!"

Jasper already had me headed in the direction of the noise coming from behind a big rhododendron bush.

"Dani. Help me get out of here before they find me. I don't trust Mick Walker."

At the same moment that I saw Sunny, crouched and hidden behind the bush, Maggie Marshall pulled her Jeep to a stop at the curb.

Mick Walker had not endeared himself to me when he'd barged in, gun drawn, while Luke and I were in Sunny's house. Now, I didn't hesitate, grabbing Sunny's arm and shoving her into Maggie's Jeep. "I'll explain later, Maggie. Take her to Sea Breeze."

Maggie, my private investigator friend and someone who was always ready for an adventure, registered a moment of surprise, then nodded and screeched off. I wasn't sure she'd be thrilled with this adventure when she learned that it interfered with her boyfriend, Detective AJ Crenshaw's investigation. He'd be furious.

I sighed with relief for Sunny. Maggie would come around when she understood the stakes.

"Come on," I said to Luke and Jasper. "We have to finish our walk before AJ puts two and two together."

"You just jumped in with both feet, Dani. I hope you know what you're doing." I couldn't tell if Luke thought I'd just made the biggest mistake of my life or performed a noble deed.

With all my heart, I hoped it was the later.

Time would tell about that.

*a*s casually as possible, I walked up the path into the Blue Moon Inn with Luke, Pip, and Jasper. I cleared my mind of my involvement with Sunny Shaw's disappearance, and braced myself for AJ's questions.

Not one to disappoint, he ambushed me just inside the entryway when I walked in. "Where is she, Dani?"

I actually jumped, letting out a squeak in surprise. Pip yipped and raised her hackles at whatever had frightened me. Jasper, not to be left out, let out a deep woof that practically shook the windows next to the front door. Luke squeezed my hand, filling me with courage and making me thankful for this support team.

I patted my chest. "Jeez Louise, AJ. What the heck are you doing scaring us half to death. And," pulling myself together, I tilted my head quizzically, "why are you still here?" My question sounded genuine even to my ears.

He studied my face with narrowed eyes.

I held his gaze without blinking once.

"Sunny Shaw. Where is she? You told her to tell Lily she had to go with me to the police station. Was that some kind of code you sent so Lily knew to stash her where I couldn't find her?"

Fortunately, I hadn't thought of that plan myself. The absurdity of Sunny being stashed away like a forgotten pair of old jeans made me laugh.

"Are you serious?" I asked. "Where exactly would Lily stash a young woman, AJ? Maybe tucked in one of her kitchen cupboards with the bread pans?"

Luke chuckled but AJ glared.

"Have you lost your teeny tiny spec of common sense that you sometimes manage to find?" Luke jabbed me with his elbow after that comment, and I knew I'd probably gone overboard. However, I'd known AJ for my whole life, and he never showed an abundance of common sense.

It wasn't just steam coming out of AJ's ears now,

his eyes practically glowed red. Let him fume for all I cared.

We stared at each other. I refused to let Detective AJ Crenshaw intimidate me.

Fortunately, since my eyes were getting kind of dry, AJ blinked first. He pointed at me, jabbing his finger with each word. "This isn't over. I'll find Sunny and when I do—"

"What, AJ?" I just couldn't keep my comments to myself. "Sunny Shaw is free to come and go as she pleases. Unless you have something to charge her with? You can't hold her against her will."

"We'll see about that." With one last angry glare, he walked out and slammed the door.

I gave my hands a big swipe, brushing AJ out of my system for now.

Lily peeked around the door with question marks in her eyes.

"Now what, Dani?" Luke asked. "You've drawn a line in the sand.

I acknowledged Luke's comment with a nod but didn't have a plan to deal with his, *what now*. Yet. "Did Sunny find you in the kitchen a little bit ago, Lil?"

"That's what AJ asked me, too. No, I didn't see her. What's going on? I get the feeling something big just happened right under my nose." She pushed the door all the way open. "Follow me before my casserole burns to a crisp."

Luke and I followed Lily and the savory aroma wafting from the kitchen. Lily picked up a spoon giving a quick stir to one of her pots before she slipped her hand into a potholder mitt and removed her casserole. "Just in time," she said. "I almost ruined everything."

Luke and I settled on stools. "This is what happened, Lil," I began. "AJ wanted Sunny to go to the police station with him. When she heard the officer from Pineville would question her, I guess she got spooked and flew the coop."

"Don't leave out the part where you shoved Sunny into Maggie's Jeep, Dani," Luke said.

The memory of Maggie's shocked expression when I pushed Sunny into her Jeep sent me into a fit of giggles. "I hope she forgives me," I managed to say in between snorts and gasps for air, "when she finds out that she helped her boyfriend's main suspect disappear into thin air. All I told her was to take Sunny to Sea Breeze. Once she finds out the rest of the story, she may never talk to me again."

"Don't worry. A murder investigation will win her over," Lily said.

"At any rate, I can't say I blame Sunny for taking off. Luke and I had the pleasure of bumping into Officer Walker at her house. At the end of his gun, no less."

"What?" Lily shrieked. "He threatened to shoot you?"

"Not exactly."

"We don't know that for sure. He had his weapon pointed right at us."

I rolled my eyes at Luke for interrupting. "And, get this, Lil," I said. "After Walker left, we couldn't find a folder belonging to Benny that Sunny asked us to bring back to her."

Lily leaned on the counter, her eyes growing larger. "He took it?" she asked, following every word.

I couldn't share these details with AJ, of course, so I appreciated her interest. "We don't know, but I did find this on the floor under her kitchen table." I pulled the list out of my pocket. "Here, take a look. Do any of these names ring a bell with you?"

Lily's eyebrows shot up as she ran her finger down the list of names. "Every single person on this list is coming to the brunch on Saturday. What does this mean?"

I shook my head. "I wish we knew. I think it fell out of a folder that Benny left at Sunny's house. The missing folder. By the way, is the brunch still on now that Benny is..." I tried to think of a polite way of describing his absence.

"Out of the picture?" Luke said, helping me out.

"Yes, thank goodness. It would have ruined my opening booking if they'd canceled."

A grin spread across my face. "Do you need extra help serving?"

Lily's grin matched mine. "I know what you're thinking, Dani. I *absolutely* need your help, but let's keep Sunny away out of sight, okay?"

"Out of sight or out of your inn, Lil? This morning you weren't keen on having her around. You agreed to take one day at a time."

Lily flicked her wrist dismissively. "I'm rooting for the underdog here. Besides," and I knew the real reason for her one-eighty turnaround, "she made all the windows in the guest rooms sparkle without a complaint. Then, she cleaned all the cupboards in the kitchen and smiled the whole time. Who smiles while doing those kind of chores?"

"So, what you're trying to say in your roundabout way, Lily, is that Dani was right to bring Sunny over here?" Luke asked.

Lily gently punched my arm. "No, that's not what I meant. Sunny was a help this morning, but whether you were right or wrong to bring her here," she waffled her hand back and forth, "is yet to be determined."

"Nuff said you two." Luke inserted himself between our silly banter. "Dani, you have to deal with Sunny and Maggie at our house before something goes off the rails. Specifically, why was she outside hiding in the bushes?"

"If she took off because of that police officer, she needs to stay away from here," I said.

"Or behind a closed door and out of sight. She's the link between Benny and the others," Luke said, always adding common sense insight.

"Keep this in mind, Lil. Luke and I talked briefly with Officer Walker and Hunter Bodane, the owner of Nine Pine Nurseries. They both knew that Sunny was going out with Benny on his boat this morning."

"That's nothing on its own... unless they had a motive to kill him."

"Right," I said. "And that's what we have to figure out." I slid off the stool. "Luke, let's go talk to Sunny. I'm sure she's frantic to get back together with Jasper."

"She won't fit in your little MG, Dani."

"No problem," Lily said. "Take my SUV. It's parked out back. And be careful," she warned.

13

*L*ily walked outside ahead of us to pamper my paranoia. She checked to see if any cars were watching the front of the inn. With a killer on the loose, I couldn't be too careful.

She put one thumb up. "All's clear," She said and waved us out. "And take this." She handed Luke a casserole still warm and fragrant while I corralled Jasper and Pip. "It's a thank you for all of Sunny's help."

I kissed Lily's cheek and said, "I'll tell her. We'll all chip in to help make your first event a big success despite the murder."

"Don't forget about the clam chowder, Dani. I'm counting on you."

"Sure thing." Lily gave the key to her SUV to

Luke, and I let the dogs climb in the back, then ran around to the passenger seat. "Let's go, Luke," I said, eager to get on our way.

He started the SUV and shot me a grin. "I told Lily to walk out to your car and put something inside to foil AJ while I take this old unused exit that cuts over to a side street. I'm convinced your detective friend will have someone keeping an eye on you after Sunny disappeared. I don't think he believed your innocent act for one second."

"Good thinking," I said as the SUV jumped over a couple of rocks and a pile of brush on the road before we reached the pavement again.

"Duck down, just in case," Luke said when we hit Main Street.

"Are you serious? You really think we have to do all this cloak and dagger stuff?" I leaned over so my head rested against Luke's arm out of sight. Of course, if anyone was watching they'd see Jasper's big head in the back window and Pip looking out the opposite one. Two dead giveaways for sure.

Luke laughed and put his arm around me. "Naw," he said. "I just wanted you nice and close."

I liked that part, I had to admit. I snuggled a little closer until Luke slammed on the brakes, and I almost smashed my head into the steering wheel.

"What?"

He held my head down with his hand. "AJ just drove by but he didn't slow down, so I think we're good. I'll take a side street. It'll take a bit longer but I'd rather not risk having him see us."

"Do you think he's been watching the inn? Does he have time for that?"

Without answering, Luke threw a baseball cap onto my lap. "You can sit up now. But put this on. It might help a little."

I guessed that was my answer.

I tucked my auburn curls under the cap and scooched down, keeping as low a profile on the seat as possible. "Luke," I said looking up, "if AJ or someone else is keeping tabs on me, do you think it's to find Sunny?"

"Why else, Dani? Have you gotten involved in something that you haven't told me about yet?" Luke glanced at me with his eyebrows raised.

"Very funny."

He sped up now that we were out of the Misty Harbor town limits. "At this point, she's the best link to Benny that they have. With the fear we saw in her eyes when AJ mentioned Officer Walker's name, I'm worried that she might be in serious danger herself."

We zipped along the twisty road that gave

glimpses of Blueberry Bay, but today, I barely registered the stunning scenery in my impatience to get to Sea Breeze.

Finally, Luke turned into our entryway, and I sighed with relief as we passed between the granite markers. I could relax now and work on this mystery. But it wouldn't be easy. We'd barely begun unraveling this crazy maze.

I grabbed Lily's casserole and let the dogs out of the back seat.

Jasper hesitated.

Pip yipped as if she was telling Jasper that we were safely home because the big dog jumped out and followed my little Pipsqueak to the front door.

"That Pip is something else," Luke said. "She's taken to her big friend like a momma bird with a misfit chick." He shook his head at the pair. "At least, with Jasper, you don't have to find a new home for her like you did for some of the other four-legged dogs that fell in your lap."

I looked at Pip and remembered how she ended up living with me after her owner was murdered. I opened the door. Pip dashed inside followed by Jasper at a more lumbering pace.

"Jasper!" I heard Sunny screech with excitement as we entered my kitchen. She wrapped her arms around the massive head and whispered something into her dog's ear.

I slid the casserole onto the counter. "Lily sent this along to thank you for all your help this morning," I said. "She raved about your hard work and pleasant attitude. You made quite an impression."

"Dani?" Maggie said, in a stern voice.

Oh, right. I'd forgotten about Maggie. I sensed a scolding headed my way. She sat glowering at me from the kitchen nook with a mug of coffee in front of her.

"Hi, Mags."

She tapped her nails on the mug—click, click, click. "Sunny told me about her adventure this morning." More clicks. "What have you dragged me into?" Maggie's tone took a turn, decidedly unfriendly now. She pointed a finger at me. "You know AJ probably won't talk to me after that stunt, and just when we were getting along so well."

Maggie's definition of getting along well meant something a whole lot different than mine. The two of them still couldn't agree they each had adorable kittens. Oh no. One had to be smarter, or cuter, or more physical. I'd never understand their need for outdoing each other.

I scooped a big helping of the lobster macaroni

onto a plate and set it in front of Maggie. Her weakness for food in general was dwarfed only by her love for lobster in particular. I wondered if Lily knew I'd need her casserole to placate Maggie. Probably.

"Just for you," I said and slid into the chair opposite her. The aroma even tickled my taste buds. Would the deliciousness tempt Maggie? More importantly, would it soften her mood so we could get down to the business at hand?

"A bribe, Dani?" Maggie eyed me suspiciously. "I know how you use food to get what you want." She stuck her fork into a big piece of lobster.

"*Moi*?" I said with my best, innocent puppy dog eyes. "This is straight from Lily." I cupped my hand around my mouth. "She sent it over for Sunny," I shrugged, "but it's really for sharing."

Maggie moved her fork with the tender morsel to her mouth.

I tried not to smile, but I felt the edge of my lips twitch.

"I saw that," she said. "Just because I'm eating this doesn't mean I'm not still angry with you."

"Of course, Mags. I understand." I folded my hands chastely on the table and bit my lips.

Jasper picked this perfect moment to walk over to Maggie and lay her big head on her lap.

Maggie looked down. "For crying out loud. This isn't fair. How can I ignore those pleading eyes?" She set her fork down and worked her fingers in Jasper's soft fur. "You and Sunny need my help?" she cooed to Jasper. "Okay."

I was pretty sure that Jasper had only been hoping for something to fall off Maggie's fork, but I could live with this other interpretation, too. Maybe when Sunny whispered in her dog's ear, she'd told her to beg for Maggie's help.

Who knew?

Dogs, in my experience, had common sense smarts we couldn't understand, and mysterious gifts of insight. And maybe this dog, in particular, knew an important detail about the murderer that she'd share when the time was right.

14

As we sat at my kitchen nook—Maggie on her second helping of Lily's mac and cheese, Luke chatting with my grandma, Rose, and Sunny gazing out the window at Blueberry Bay—I worried about where this murder investigation would lead.

I studied Sunny's sad expression as she looked away in an unguarded moment. What thoughts were going through her head?

"Sunny?" I said hoping to gently pull her back to the present.

She jerked her head in my direction.

"You haven't touched your food."

A wan smile flitted across her lips as she poked her fork into the food. "I guess I'm just not very hungry. This morning's shock is hitting me really hard right now for some reason."

"Oh, honey," Rose said, tenderly stroking Sunny's cheek, "of course you're having a tough time. You've been through a terrible ordeal, losing your friend and fleeing for your life. No one is ever prepared for something like that."

Maggie scratched her head, and I could tell she had something she wanted to add to the conversation but for some reason she held back. "Just spit it out, Mags," I said.

"Well," she pushed away from the table and leaned back in her chair, probably to make more room for all the food she'd shoveled in. "We could help you, Sunny. The way I see it, the police in Misty Harbor and Pineville are teaming up to get to the bottom of the murder. It could mean one of two things."

"Both bad from my perspective," Sunny said sounding miserable.

"They might just want every detail you can remember, including insight into Benny's possible enemies."

"Or?"

Maggie inhaled deeply. "Or, they found evidence that puts you at the top of their suspect list."

"If they even have a suspect list with more than one name," Sunny mumbled.

"Speaking about lists," I said as I remembered the paper in my pocket. "What do you make of this?" I smoothed out the paper I'd found in Sunny's house and slid it across to her.

She studied it. "Where did this come from?" she asked, a wrinkle forming between her eyebrows.

"I found it under your kitchen table."

"I've never seen it before." She flipped it over, but the back was blank. "It's a list of the people Benny was preparing to speak to at the brunch at the Blue Moon Inn."

I nodded; glad she'd confirmed what Lily had told me. "Do you know anything about these people?" I asked. I got up to put water on for tea while Luke got a pot of coffee going.

"I wouldn't say I know any of them well, but I do know some of them, and I've heard of all of them." She shoved her food around absent-mindedly, still not actually eating any of it.

"Like Mick Walker, right?" I asked. "When I found you hiding in the bushes you said you didn't trust him. Why, Sunny?" After one meeting with the Pineville cop, I wasn't a big fan of him either, but I wanted to know what happened between him and

Sunny to make her run when his name was mentioned?

"It's hard to explain," Sunny started to say, but hesitated and didn't seem to know how to continue. "Mick is just someone that makes me uncomfortable. Plus, there was no love lost between Benny and Mick. I guess that's why I took off when your town detective said Mick wanted to talk to me. Benny always stood between us when Mick got, kind of, you know—"

"Too friendly?" I offered since she was having trouble finding the right word. "Benny likes you, doesn't he," I said. "Luke and I went to the Nine Pine Nursery and that's what Hunter Bodane told us." I poured hot water into my teapot, and Luke carried the coffee to the table. I hunted in my cupboard, glad to find a tin filled with chocolate chip oatmeal cookies. They weren't fresh from the oven, but they'd do.

"You talked to Hunter?" Sunny asked and poured herself some mint tea from my teapot. "He knew Benny and I were going out on the boat this morning."

Maggie snagged herself a cookie and a mug of coffee. "Did this Hunter guy have any reason to want Benny dead?" she asked, straight to the point, before devouring her cookie.

"I don't think so," Sunny answered and stifled a yawn. "They've been friends for as long as I've known them. Benny was frustrated. He was trying to help Hunter save his greenhouse business with new branding and promotional ideas so Hunter wouldn't feel forced to sell. But Benny said that Hunter was only lukewarm at best to those ideas. He was afraid that Hunter had made up his mind to sell his property outright to the top bidder instead of saving it or putting it into a conservation restriction. Conserving the property was Benny's top priority."

"That could have upset plenty of people," Maggie said. "If the land is worth developing, I'd imagine someone has their eye on bankrolling it."

Rose stood up, effectively ending the discussion. "I suppose we have a guest for the night?" she asked me. "I for one need a good night's sleep before we delve into all this any further, and I'm sure Sunny is exhausted after her ordeal."

"I don't want to cause you any trouble," Sunny said. "I thought I was supposed stay at the Blue Moon Inn."

"That was the plan, right, Dani?" Luke said, but I refused to look at him. Surely, he knew the inn wouldn't work if AJ was keeping an eye out for Sunny's return.

"How about she stays with you, Maggie? AJ would never expect to find her at his girlfriend's place," I said, patting myself on the back for such a clever plan.

Maggie's jaw dropped, almost hitting her chest. "Are you serious? You already put me in enough potential trouble with him if he finds out you shoved Sunny into my Jeep. No offense, Sunny, but I'm not sure I'll have any chance of saving my relationship with AJ if I harbor his suspect."

Sunny solved the problem for us. "I'm going to stay at the Blue Moon Inn," she said. "I promised to help Lily and I keep my word." She left no room for argument, and I had to hand it to her, she had spunk and determination, plus that special ingredient —trustworthiness.

"If AJ comes looking for me there, fine. I don't mind talking to him again, I just was caught completely off guard when I heard Officer Walker's name."

"Fair enough," I said. "Mick Walker didn't impress me one bit when he showed up at your house with his gun drawn on us."

"He what?" Sunny said. She lurched forward in her chair. "What was he doing at my house?"

"I'm not sure. I saw your neighbor spying on us,

and I assumed she called the police when she saw strangers going into your house."

Sunny laughed out loud. "Tilly? Let me tell you all a secret. Tilly Morris is my pistol-packing guardian grannie. She's not my real grannie, mind you. She adopted me when I moved in. Anyway, I sent her a message and told her I wouldn't be home for a few days, and someone was stopping by to pick up clothes for me. She'd *never* call the police to my house. She knows what I think about Mick Walker, and she'd more likely arrive waving her weapon and screeching like a banshee if she thought I needed help."

We all stared open-mouthed at Sunny. Wow! Tilly could teach Maggie a thing or two.

"I wonder if Officer Walker had already staked out your house, Sunny. And was waiting for you to return."

Color drained from her face, and she reached to pull Jasper closer. "If that's true, Dani, maybe he's the one who took Benny's folder. I bet that list you found on the floor slipped out of it. Benny was always thorough when he prepared for a presentation. He would have had notes on everyone's background so he could target his comments and push for conservation to have the most impact."

Maggie picked up the list, folded it, and tucked it in her pocket. "I'm heading home. One thing I'm good at is digging up information. Let me see what I can turn up on these names."

"Something that got him killed," Luke said. "Be careful, Maggie."

She grinned. "This is my kind of fun. Want a lift, Sunny? I brought you here, I may as well take you back."

"And Jasper, too?"

"Of course. Jasper, too. I'll even walk you inside to make sure no one is waiting to ambush you."

Luke gathered up the dishes while I walked with Maggie and Sunny to the door.

"Come to the diner for breakfast in the morning, and we can make a plan," I said.

I couldn't abandon Sunny now. She needed friends now more than ever. Friends who believed her since it sure looked like others out there might think she shouldn't talk to anyone.

15

I tossed and turned through the night until I just gave up and rolled out of bed as the sun peeked above the horizon. Tiptoeing quietly so as not to disturb Luke, Pip and I went downstairs. A hot cup of tea called to me even though Pip scratched at the French door telling me she was ready for a jog on the beach.

"First thing first, Pipster," I told her.

With my tea in hand, I knocked on the door leading to Rose's apartment and poked my head in. "Are you up?" I asked even though I knew she was always up at the crack of dawn.

"Come on in," she answered. "Are you having trouble sleeping?" she asked when I curled up next to her and watched the sun spread its stunning magic over Blueberry Bay.

Her cat, Trouble, eyed me suspiciously before he settled back on Rose's lap with his tail curled around his face. Pip knew enough to give the ornery cat plenty of space.

"Yes," I said in answer to Rose's question. "I keep thinking about Officer Walker showing up at Sunny's house. Was it over the top to come in like that with his gun drawn on us? I mean, was he just being careful or was something else going on?"

"Like what?"

"Well, I'm not sure, but according to Sunny, Benny's folder was in her house. Who else knew about it? What information was in it? Maybe Officer Walker thought that's what we, or someone else was after."

"Which means he knew about the folder," Rose said. "I had the impression that Benny was more careful than to blab about his work. Especially if he left it with Sunny. Who would know to look for it there?"

"That's the million-dollar question, isn't it?" I said. "Benny thought he was in some kind of danger since he told Sunny to find me if anything happened to him. That in itself was odd. But considering that situation, it makes perfect sense that he wouldn't leave all his work laying around in his own house. But it was short-sighted for him to think it would be safe with Sunny if worst came to worst."

Rose stroked Trouble who purred with contentment. "The fact that someone murdered him suggests that the killer wanted to stop him from presenting his findings. They figured out they had to uncover every rock to find his report. Including Sunny's house. If you're committed to helping her, you've got your work cut out, Danielle. Is that your plan?"

I knew what she was doing. She wanted me to be sure that I knew what I was jumping into, danger and all. "It is," I said. "Something happened on that boat yesterday morning, and I'm afraid Sunny is in more danger than she realizes. She needs our help."

"Which puts you in danger, too. Once you start asking questions, someone will try to stop you," Rose said.

"That's why Pip stays with me all the time, right Pipster?" And, of course, she yipped her agreement since Pip didn't shy away from any adventure whether it had danger written on it or not.

I stood up and twisted from side to side. "We're going for a jog on the beach in case Luke comes looking for us. And then I told Maggie to meet me at the diner. I hope she dug up some good information to get us headed in the right direction to help Sunny."

Rose waved us off from her cozy spot with a view of the beach. It was nice to know that she'd watch over us as we jogged. Maybe she wasn't a pistol-toting grannie like Tilly Morris, but Rose always had my back. And that gave me confidence to push myself.

Outside, I managed to do a few more stretches before Pip lost patience with me and headed down the steps to the beach. She charged at the breaking waves and disturbed some seagulls resting on the sand. They flew off, squawking their displeasure. Yup, this was my life—Blueberry Bay, with waves, seagulls, and a briny mist—and I loved it.

I followed Pip until we reached the rocky area below the Kitty Point Lighthouse before turning back, retracing our footprints in the sand to Sea Breeze.

Luke surprised me when I walked into the kitchen. He kissed my forehead and said, "I'll, drop you at the diner on my way to Blueberry Acres. I have some chores to take care of today."

Even on a day off, some things just can't wait.

"Stay for breakfast at least and hear what Maggie uncovered," I said. "All this conservation stuff is right up your alley. Maybe it will make more sense to you."

He gave me a big grin. "You know I never turn down an invitation to eat at the Little Dog Diner." He pulled me close and rested his chin on the top of my head. "Hmmm. If I close my eyes, I can smell the salty ocean beach. I'm still not used to waking up to that treat. Ready to go?"

"I'm not sure the Little Dog Diner customers want their eggs with a hint of ocean in the next booth, so give me ten minutes to shower and change while you finish that cup of coffee."

I took the stairs two at a time and made it back in a flat eight minutes, my curls still dripping down my back but at least I smelled like meadow flowers instead of briny ocean.

"Not bad, right?" I said.

He gave me a thumbs up, and said, "Let's go."

The diner hummed while Chad and Christy hustled to get everything set for the day. The booths sparkled, ready for hungry customers. I poked my head into the kitchen where Chad had pancake batter ready, omelet ingredients prepared, and muffins cooling on the counter.

"Morning," I said. "No problems?"

"No problems," he hesitated, "but if you don't have any immediate plans, could you help out through the morning rush? Just so we don't get too backed up. I hate to ask on your day off."

"Of course. Don't give it a second thought. Our plans have been shoved to the sideline anyway," I said to Chad. "The Little Dog Diner gets my attention before anything else. Without the two of you, I'd never get a minute off. I'll be back by the time we open for business."

I found a basket and filled it with muffins.

Luke looked at me with his eyebrows raised. "What's up?"

I grabbed his arm. "Let's go up to Maggie's apartment."

"And wake her up? You know what a grouch she is in the morning," Luke said. "Maybe I'll just wait here and enjoy the peace and quiet."

"Okay. Have it your way." I held up my basket. "I have warm muffins for her so that should make her happy."

Luke grinned and shook his head. "You don't play fair you know."

"I know. And here's one for you to tide you over until I get back."

Maggie's apartment was right next door above the Blueberry Bay Grapevine. Pip and I climbed the stairs and I peeked through the glass window in the door. "Here goes, Pip. I hope she doesn't bite my head off." I rapped on the door. "Maggie, open up. I have a warm muffin for you."

Nothing.

I knocked again.

Her kitty, Radar, mewed behind the door. That would get Maggie moving.

Sure enough, she stumbled into the kitchen, hair sticking out in every direction, and glared at me. I smiled and held up the basket.

She picked up Radar and opened the door. "What are you doing here so early? I thought we were meeting for breakfast."

Without waiting for an invitation, Pip scooted through the opening and I followed. "Breakfast, right. Come on down. Luke's waiting for us. You know, we have lots to do so we need an early start."

"Okay. Okay. Let me get dressed." She took a big bite of a muffin. "Mmmm, it's still warm."

"Did you find out anything last night?" I asked hoping to get Maggie's brain working.

"I sure did." She took another bite. "You won't believe what I discovered but you'll have to wait until I have a big cheddar cheese omelet with home fries sitting in front of me. And coffee. A big pot of coffee. Then I'll be able to remember everything." She winked at me, so I knew she wasn't mad at me for waking her up. And the sugar was kicking in.

"I'm on that order for you, Mags. It'll be waiting when you arrive."

"Dani?"

I turned around to face her.

"Sunny's in a heap of trouble from what I can tell."

"Trouble or danger?"

"Probably both."

That wasn't what I wanted to hear.

16

I left Pip in Maggie's apartment to play with Radar. The two could tire each other out while I enjoyed breakfast with Luke.

In the diner, Luke informed me that he'd ordered our breakfasts, so I popped into the kitchen and added Maggie's request.

"Sure thing, Dani," Chad answered, adding home fries to the grill. I couldn't be luckier to have this hardworking couple working for me, giving me some freedom to come and go. "Here are the two breakfasts that Luke ordered. Hope you don't mind that I added sliced tomatoes with a sprig of fresh basil. The colors make everything pop on the plate. What do you think?"

"Brilliant! Don't worry about experimenting, that's how we discover what our customers love."

With the two plates in hand, I slipped in next to Luke, setting our breakfast feasts down. "Maggie's joining us. I hope you don't mind."

"As long as she has good information, I guess I'll put up with the intrusion," he teased. "She did find something, right?"

"So she says." I poured hot water over a peppermint teabag. "Here she comes. The lure of free food certainly motivates her to get her act in gear in record time."

Luke grinned as he eyed the plate in front of him. "I totally understand that." He helped himself to a big forkful of omelet, closed his eyes, and groaned with delight.

"Hey," Maggie said as she slipped in across from us. "Pip is the best kitty sitter ever, just wanted you to know that she can visit anytime."

Christy arrived with Maggie's plate. I thought I saw a bit of drool at the edge of her lips when she looked at the plate in front of her, overflowing with crispy home fries and a veggie omelet oozing cheese out one end.

"I'll be right back with that big pot of strong coffee," Christy said with a wink at me.

"So," I said as we all settled into our food. "What did you discover, Mags?"

She dabbed her lips with the napkin, "Plenty. I started with our State Senator, Matt Nash."

"Our Maine state senator?" Luke asked. "I didn't make that connection when I saw the list, did you Dani?"

I shook my head. "I should have but, no, it didn't click. What about him?" I asked. Maggie had my attention.

Christy arrived with the coffee, setting it down and leaving us to our discussion.

Maggie filled her mug. "Matt Nash organized this meeting and invited Benny Chadman to discuss the impact of, wait for it," she sipped her coffee, "a golf course where Nine Pine Nursery is now located."

"A golf course?" Luke stared at Maggie. "That land abuts Blueberry Bay. Benny must have been freaking out worrying about runoff into the ocean. Golf courses use lots of fertilizer and weed killers to keep the grass perfect."

"Too bad we didn't find his folder before someone else got their hands on it. My guess is that he was not going to give a green light to this project," I said. "What's the senator like?"

"From what I could gather," Maggie continued,

"he's well-liked, charismatic, and usually gets what he wants."

"Does he want the golf course to go forward?"

"I'm not sure. I think the purpose of the planned meeting was supposed to hash out all points of view. I suppose that's why he asked Benny to give the environmental impact side of the picture."

"Okay," I said, checking to see how much time I had before the diner was open for business. Not much. "What about Hunter Bodane?" I asked hoping to push Maggie along. "When Luke and I talked to him, he hinted about a project that he was hoping would go through. Now, I'm assuming he was talking about this golf course."

"He didn't mince his words that Benny might mess up the plan, even though he considered Benny a friend." Luke added. Done with his breakfast, he leaned back in the booth and stretched his arm along the back, catching one of my curls and twirling it around his finger.

Maggie downed the rest of her coffee and refilled her mug. "I discovered that Hunter Bodane is in some deep financial trouble. He invested a ton of money upgrading his greenhouse and equipment, but it didn't translate into much of a bump in sales.

He's in a tough spot, sitting on that piece of valuable land that's mortgaged to the bank."

I sipped my tea, taking all that in. "That explains his frustration, maybe even jealousy, that Benny had a trust fund and didn't have to work," I said. I remembered our conversation with Hunter the day before. "He was worried that Benny would throw a monkey wrench, his description, into things and mess up the project."

Maggie thumped her mug onto the table. "He said that? I'd say he had a pretty strong motive to make sure Benny didn't muck up his big sale for this golf course plan. But did he know where Benny was yesterday morning?"

"He sure did," Luke said. "He knew Benny took Sunny out on his boat. Unless he has an alibi, he's a likely suspect."

Maggie scribbled furiously and mumbled, "This is great. I love being in the middle of all the excitement."

I was getting a little fevered myself. "Did you find out anything about the Crystal person on the list, Mags?" I asked, on the edge of my seat now. "She drove into Nine Pine Nurseries while we were there, and Hunter couldn't get away from us fast enough to talk to her."

Maggie licked her finger and flipped back a few pages in her notebook. "Let me see. Crystal Tilson, assistant to Senator Matt Nash. His scheduler, spin doctor to the media, she basically shields him from anything unpleasant. She's attractive, Harvard-educated, and never gets flustered. She gets high marks for her performance."

"From watching her approach Hunter, I'd have to add she's got that extra dose of confidence that probably gets her exactly what she wants," I said. "Does she have a romantic interest?"

"That's what everyone wants to know, but she plays coy when asked. I did find some photos of Crystal with Hunter Bodane together, always out of town at fancy restaurants or in Boston at a concert or other event." Maggie raised a shoulder. "I don't know, they could just be friends."

From what I'd observed, Hunter's face lit up when Crystal arrived at his business. I'd say *he'd* like it to be more than a friendship. I slid out of the booth. "I'd better get in the kitchen before my two fantastic employees go on strike. They need some help through the breakfast rush, then I'll pop up to your apartment. Okay, Maggie?"

"No, let's meet at the inn. Sunny might have more details to add to these profiles. I think it's important that we keep an eye on her anyway. But don't tell her I said that. I don't want her to disappear thinking that would keep her safe."

"Safe from what?" The image of Officer Walker with his gun aimed at Luke and me flashed across my memory bank, but was there something else Maggie had unearthed?

"That's the problem, Dani. Sunny is the link and if we're right to assume that one of the people coming to the meeting at the Blue Moon Inn is a murderer, they might think she knows more than she's told us."

"Okay. The Blue Moon Inn as soon as I can get away. Keep digging, Mags."

Before I was out of earshot, Maggie said, "One more thing, Dani."

From her tone, I knew this one more thing was a new twist.

"Sunny's grandparents used to own the Nine Pine Nursery.

I hadn't seen that coming.

17

*A*fter Luke and Maggie left the diner, I unlocked the front door for business. AJ, my first customer, strode in wearing a scowl. What a way to start the day I thought but put on my best cheerful how-can-I-help you voice. "Good morning."

Without skipping a beat, AJ replied, "Black coffee, a blueberry muffin, and we need to talk, Dani." He continued past me and settled into the booth farthest from the door.

Not exactly pleased with a summons like that without even the courtesy of a hello or good morning to soften the command, I wanted to get this over and done with as quickly as possible. Grabbing his coffee and muffin, I returned before he'd even had time to remove his hat.

"Here you go, one black coffee and a muffin filled with juicy blueberries." Silently, I hoped this might soften his dark mood.

"Sit down, Dani."

I glanced around the diner. Customers began to fill up the counter stools and booths. Friendly chatter was a welcome background filler, together with mugs sliding on the counter and silverware clinking against plates. I'd give him a few minutes.

"I came first thing before you get swamped." AJ pointed to the seat across from him. "It's important."

I sat.

"Why did Sunny take off when I mentioned Officer Walker's name yesterday?" Without taking his eyes off me, he stirred his coffee. It was an odd gesture with no added sugar or cream unless his goal was to cool it down a bit. "Please don't insult my intelligence by claiming ignorance."

"Here's the thing, AJ," I said, knowing there was no point in skirting the issue. "Sunny doesn't trust Officer Walker."

He nodded and relaxed slightly, leaning across the table to get as close to me as possible. "Walker was furious yesterday when I returned to the station and said I couldn't find her. So mad, in fact, that I was glad she'd disappeared."

I didn't expect that, and AJ must have seen the shocked look on my face.

"You heard me right. In my opinion, something is off with that guy." He bit into his muffin, making me wait until he'd enjoyed half of the treat. "I know you, Dani. You can't help but poke around in something like this. And you know that I can't tell you any details, but what I *can* say is this—Sunny stumbled into something big. She needs to be really careful. Okay?"

I heard the urgency in his voice, sending a chill up my spine. "Thanks, AJ." I wasn't sure what he'd discovered but this warning on top of what Maggie said, didn't take a rocket scientist to understand. Sunny, and now I, by default, were involved in something unsavory at best, dangerous for sure, and possibly deadly at worst. "Are you telling me that she's not a suspect now?"

"She can leave town if she wants to," he said which didn't exactly answer what I'd asked, but I'd take it. "But I don't think it's a good idea for her to go to her house by herself." AJ raised one eyebrow. "Do you understand what I mean?"

I put my hand over AJ's. "I understand loud and clear. For what it's worth, Sunny said she doesn't mind talking to you if you have more questions. I don't think she's hiding anything. To be honest, I think she's scared out of her mind. Can I ask you a question?"

AJ sat back and grinned like I'd just told him a joke. "Dani, you can always ask anything you want to, but I can't promise to answer."

"Fair enough. I'm sure you know that Benny was invited to speak at the Blue Moon Inn. Lily told me the meeting is still on. Just recently, I learned that a golf course is planned on a piece of property in Pineville."

AJ nodded. I guessed he already knew these details. He waited for me to continue.

"Benny was against the golf course plan. His speech would address the environmental impact on Blueberry Bay. If he'd discovered a negative impact, that could put him at odds with those at the meeting supporting the golf course. *I* think one of those people didn't want him to share that information. Is that the track you're on, too?"

AJ considered my question. "I have to keep an open mind but that certainly is something we are looking into."

"Fair enough, I'll take that as a yes."

His smile told me everything I needed to know. "Hey, what's Maggie been up to? She wasn't at her apartment when I stopped by yesterday late afternoon." He finished his coffee but kept a close eye on me. He had to suspect that with me involved with Sunny's problems, there was a good chance Maggie was in on it, too.

"Oh, she stopped at Sea Breeze."

"By herself?" His lip twitched at the corner.

I couldn't interpret whether it was a twitch of annoyance or of humor. For all I knew, he was setting a trap hoping to catch me in a lie.

"Actually AJ, Maggie was with Rose and Sunny."

He shook his head. "You two will be the death of me, but this time I think it was a smart move for Sunny to make herself scarce. I can't say more than that, but I'm trying to get to the bottom of something that's fishier than your chowder."

He grabbed his hat and slid out of the booth, leaving a ten under the coffee mug. "Thanks for your time. Looks like it's getting busy in here now, so I'll get out of the way." He lowered his voice. "Keep your ears open. Everyone will have a theory about what happened yesterday on Blueberry Bay. Sometimes there's truth to be found in gossip."

I watched AJ walk out. We had a prickly relationship but an honest one. He didn't resist my presence on his cases as much as he used to; maybe he'd gotten used to my tendency to show up in the middle of the latest mystery whether I wanted to or not.

This time, I sure didn't want to.

*a*fter the morning rush calmed down, my friend, Sue Ellen Baer, swept into the diner wearing her latest flashy outfit.

"Morning, Sue Ellen," I said, trying not to laugh.

"What?" she asked. Apparently, I didn't do a very good job of hiding the smirk on my face.

"Nothing." I tried to look serious when I asked, "Are you wearing red *yoga* pants?"

She skimmed her hands down her thighs as if to show off her new figure. "Yes, and don't look so shocked, Dani. It's my latest activity. And, I have to say how surprised I was at all the stretching and twisting. The teacher claimed the course was gentle yoga, but it felt more like a torture chamber. I didn't know she would try to turn this body into a pretzel. Now, I need something sweet to reward myself for all my hard work."

From her comments, I wondered if Sue Ellen had any idea what yoga was before she signed up for the course. Well, she did have yoga pants. Maybe that was the most important accessory.

She walked to the glass pastry display and tapped her finger on her lips. From the way she waffled back and forth, I wondered if it was a new yoga move. "There are just too many delicious looking choices. Every one of them tempt me, Dani. What should I try?"

"Take a seat at the counter and I'll surprise you. How does that sound?" Sue Ellen would like anything I put in front of her. I could close my eyes and chose one at random.

"Perfect, as long as the surprise tastes limey... with whipped cream and a graham cracker crust, okay?"

I chuckled at her description. "I think that narrows the choice down to this." I slid a generous slice of key lime pie onto a plate. "And a glass of water to rehydrate, Sue Ellen?"

"Water? Are you crazy?" She grimaced. "I need one of your mocha coffees with an extra dollop of whipped cream and a teeny shake of chocolate sprinkles on top... you know, to make it pretty."

I hoped she wasn't expecting any weight loss from her yoga class if this was how she planned to reward herself. Not that it mattered, but I didn't want her to be disappointed and drop out, blaming the yoga.

"Here you go, Sue Ellen." I checked my watch, glad to see the diner thinning out so I'd be able to leave shortly.

"Are you getting ready to leave?" Sue Ellen pointed her fork at my watch.

"Actually, I'm heading over to the Blue Moon Inn. I found someone to help Lily for a few days, and I want to be sure it's working out." I didn't want to get too specific about Sunny's situation with other people eavesdropping on our conversation.

"What a coincidence," Sue Ellen said. She carefully set her coffee cup on its saucer. "I chatted with someone at the end of the yoga class who was heading to the Blue Moon Inn to be sure everything is all set for a meeting tomorrow. She came early to get the feel of the town."

My ears pricked up. "Did you get her name?"

Sue Ellen narrowed her eyes, letting me know she thought my question was ridiculous. "You know me better than to ask *that*, Danielle. If nothing else, I'm always polite and welcoming to someone new in town."

I couldn't argue with that comment. Sue Ellen's welcoming nature usually procured all kinds of juicy information. "I introduced myself, and she reciprocated. Crystal Wilson couldn't wait to tell me that she's the assistant to State Senator Matt Nash in a snobby superior kind of way. Well, la-di-da, I thought to myself as she packed up her yoga mat and sashayed out of class."

Another name on Benny's list. How interesting and convenient that she'd be at the Blue Moon Inn. If I hurried, maybe I could accidentally bump into her.

"Want to come with me, Sue Ellen?"

She scraped the last bits of graham cracker crumbs off her plate before she slid off the stool and grinned conspiratorially. "I thought you'd never ask."

With Chad and Christy all set for the rest of the day, I took Sue Ellen's arm. "First I have to get Pip out of Maggie's apartment, then we can walk to the inn."

"Walk?" Sue Ellen sounded absolutely horrified.

"It's not far and walking will help stretch your twisted muscles," I added before she could whine about her aching body.

Pip and Radar were curled up together on Maggie's couch when I tiptoed inside. Pip immediately perked up and carefully extricated herself from around the exhausted kitten. She dashed down the stairs straight to Sue Ellen who greeted her with her special brand of doggie talk.

"Oh, Pippy, here you go." Sue Ellen dug into her enormous leather tote bag and handed her a dog bone. "I'll have to take you to the next yoga class so you can put that teacher to shame with your downward dog thingamajig position."

"Sue Ellen?" I said as we began walking to the Blue Moon Inn. "I didn't see you yesterday, but I assume you heard through the grapevine about the murder on Blueberry Bay."

Sue Ellen's tote bag swung between us as we crossed the street, "It's all everyone is talking about," she said, "especially Crystal. I was actually relieved when the class started, or I'd still be sitting on my mat wishing she'd lose her voice so my ears would get a break. She has such a shrill voice. Anyway, she said the victim's friend, who was on the boat with him, disappeared. I wonder what happened to her."

I pulled Sue Ellen closer to me so the pedestrians near us wouldn't hear me. "That person,

Sunny Shaw, showed up in my office yesterday... wet, scared, and without a friend in town."

Sue Ellen stopped dead in her tracks. "No. Where is she now?"

I glanced toward the Blue Moon Inn.

"Bless your heart, Dani." Understanding bloomed across her face. "You're in the middle of this murder investigation, aren't you?"

A man was murdered.

His friend was in danger.

I looked at Sue Ellen. "I'm committed to helping Sunny Shaw. It's going to be difficult and dangerous, but she needs someone on her side."

19

*T*he woof that greeted us when I opened the door at Lily's inn was more like the roar of a cannon blast than a dog's greeting.

Sue Ellen jumped behind me. "What the heck is that, Daniele? I think I just wet myself."

Pip rushed inside, jumping up to lick Jasper's nose.

"Quick!" I said, "Dig out a couple more of those dog treats from your bag before she helps herself."

Sue Ellen clutched her giant tote to her chest with a look of panic on her face.

"I'm kidding, Sue Ellen. This giant Newfoundland, Jasper, is a sweetie. She's all bark and no bite, but seriously, she'll love you forever if you share your treats with her."

"Is everything okay, here?" Lily joined us in the entryway, drying her hands on an apron. "Jasper, you're not supposed to be out here. Did you push through the door again?"

Jasper wagged her plumy tail, obviously loving all the attention.

Lily closed the door behind her. "An unexpected visitor showed up," she said in a hushed voice.

I patted the one hundred plus pounds of dog leaning against me, bracing myself before she knocked me over. "Someone by the name of Crystal?" I asked.

"How'd you know?" Lily cracked the door to the sitting room open and peeked through. She nodded her head and said, "She's in there on a phone call so talk quietly."

Sue Ellen searched in her tote as Jasper stared at her with stars in her eyes. "I bumped into Crystal after my yoga class," she said. "You know me, I got her name, phone number, and even her weight. Haha... just kidding about her weight."

Sue Ellen finally pulled her hand out of her bag and tentatively held a dog bone toward Jasper. The big dog gently accepted the treat.

"She *is* polite," Sue Ellen said as she looked at her hand and wiggled her fingers. "I didn't lose any, but all that *drool*." She wiped her hand back and forth on her yoga pants, removing the slobber.

Lily screwed up her face in a disbelieving grin at Sue Ellen's disregard for her new apparel. "Dani, how about you take Sue Ellen, Jasper, and Pip back to my office. Maggie and Sunny are expecting you. If you want, bring a plate of cookies and a pot of tea into the sitting room in a few minutes. That way you can hear what Crystal has to say. It won't look too obvious, will it?"

Sue Ellen dismissed that concern with a wave of her hand, and the rattle of her bracelets filled the little foyer. "Throw on an apron, Dani, and Crystal will take one look at you and think your Lily's lowly kitchen help."

"Sue Ellen!" Lily said, though I don't know why our friend's blunt assessment of the human race would shock her after all this time.

"Take it from me, I know her type," Sue Ellen said. "She doesn't spend her valuable time analyzing the help."

"Perfect," I said. "I was wondering how I'd meet her without making my interest in her too obvious." I took Jasper's collar. "Come on you big lug. Let's get you someplace where you won't be in the way."

Sunny leaped off her chair when we walked into the office and gave Jasper a big hug. "I didn't see her sneak out of here, but I heard her bark. Did she get into trouble?"

I waved my hand dismissively. "Naw. She just gave Sue Ellen a hearty greeting. They're best friends now, right Sue Ellen? She shared a dog bone, and Jasper shared her slobber."

Sunny giggled. "Oh, she has plenty of that to go around when she decides she likes you." She held her hand out toward Sue Ellen. "Hi. I'm Sunny Shaw, Blueberry Bay's escape artist. Thanks to Jasper and Dani."

Sue Ellen plopped onto a chair. "Bless your heart, Sunny. I'm Sue Ellen. Now I think I need to hear all about your escapade while Dani plies Crystal with cookies."

"Crystal's here?" All the color in Sunny's face drained away. "Why?"

"Getting to know the feel of the town and make sure everything is all set for some meeting tomorrow. Why?" Sue Ellen asked. "You look like she's about to take you hostage, Sunny."

I was about to leave but waited to hear what this was about.

"Crystal is Senator Matt Nash's secretary," Sunny said.

Sue Ellen eyed the jar of chocolate candy on Lily's desk as she said, "*Assistant* to State Senator Matt Nash is what she told me." Maybe she'd worked up an appetite on the walk over to the inn. "I guess she thinks that sounds more important," she said, rolling her eyes as if some people thought way too much of themselves.

"Whatever she calls herself," Sunny said, "*Benny* told me that she organized this meeting. She got the ball rolling with the senator. She invited all the participants, and it was her idea to ask Benny to do the environmental impact study on behalf of the senator."

Some pieces started to click into place for me. "If she invited Benny, maybe she's not too thrilled with the golf course idea and was hoping he'd stop it," I speculated.

"Maybe," Sunny said, her eyes growing sad. "But I have to wonder why she kept such close tabs on him. She *knew* he was going out on his boat yesterday to get more photos." Tears filled her eyes, but she turned away to hide them.

"Have you ever met her?" I asked.

She sniffled and swiped her eyes before turning

back to face me. "Oh, yeah, and Crystal looked right down her perfect little nose at me. Benny said the only reason she hooked up with Senator Matt Nash was to meet all the right people and move up the political ladder to a more influential position in the government."

Maggie's pen flew across the page of her notebook as she recorded all this information. She flipped to a clean page.

"So, let me get this straight." I leaned against the doorframe. "Officer Walker and Hunter Bodane knew Benny was going out on his boat, and now Sunny says Crystal also knew that detail. Do either of *them* have a boat?" I looked at Sunny. If any of us knew that detail it would be her.

Maggie piped up. "One person we haven't talked about yet is Josh Whiting, the developer interested in turning that property into a golf course. I had to dig deep to find that tidbit." She tapped her pen against her cheek and gave us a very satisfied smile. "Guess what Mr. Whiting owns?"

"Golf clubs?" I asked.

"Probably that too, but that's not what could get the killer to Benny's boat," Maggie said. "No, according to information on Mr. Whiting's own website, he owns a cigarette boat. Apparently, besides golf, he loves speeding through the waves."

Now we were getting some place. "Incredible work, Maggie. It's time for me to head out to Lily's sitting room to see why Crystal is *really* here a day ahead of the brunch. Come on, Pip, you might come in handy."

20

I balanced Lily's silver tray carefully so I wouldn't spill a drop of tea onto the plate of tempting cookies. Since my hands were full, I pushed the door with my shoulder and entered the sitting room backwards, hearing, I assumed, Crystal speaking.

"And I'll be running the meeting now. Benny's death sure has turned into a big inconvenience for me."

An inconvenience? My blood boiled over, and I clenched the edge of the tray to restrain myself from throwing the whole thing at this prim and proper self-centered woman. I'd never even met Benny Chadman and Crystal's attitude shocked me beyond belief. Hold on, I told myself, your job is to figure out how to make this situation work for you. And Sunny.

Forcing a smile, I turned around and asked, "Tea anyone?" before I set the tray on the coffee table between Crystal and Lily.

My overly-friendly tone made me gag a little. I wondered if I'd overdone it. Lily gave me an eye roll when Crystal diverted her attention to the cookies. That let me know that *she'd* heard my touch of snark. Fortunately, Crystal wouldn't know this fake tone from my real one.

Crystal sat back on the couch, crossed her legs and nibbled on one of Lily's crisp, buttery mint cookies.

"So," she said, turning to me and brushing crumbs off her pants onto Lily's spotless floor, "you own the Little Dog Diner, don't you?"

There went my hope for flying below the radar. "Have you been to the diner?" I asked without actually answering her question as I perched on the arm of the couch.

"Actually, I did a little research after Hunter told me you'd stopped by his nursery. It looks like a cute enough place." She cocked her head, raising her eyes questioningly. I think she hoped I'd blabber about my visit to Nine Pine Nursery.

Cute enough? Is that how she expected to get me to help her, slamming my diner with faint praise? I ignored her, lavishing my attention on Pip. Crystal could play her hand before I'd give her anything.

She fidgeted for a moment and then flashed a crafty grin. "You went to Sunny's house." Well, didn't that spread around Pineville like wildfire?

I remained quiet. Her jaw muscles worked in frustration. I supposed she'd love to yell at me, but instead, she maintained her professional persona. "One of the reasons I'm in town a day ahead of the *senator's meeting...* " she paused to let that important detail sink in, "is to talk to Sunny. No one seems to know where she is? Do you?"

"I do."

Crystal's eyes bugged out. I'd wager that as the *senator's assistant*, she wasn't used to people giving her a hard time. "Like I said, I'd like to talk to her," she repeated, as though she thought I was a moron.

I shot her a cool look and said, "Sunny had a traumatic experience this morning. I'll ask her to give you a call when she feels up to talking. What's your number?"

"My number?" she said incredulously.

"You know, your cell phone number. So she can call you? Someone of your importance must have it at your fingertips. You know, in case the *senator* needs to get in touch with you."

Crystal shot daggers at me. "I want to talk to her *now*. I can't wait for her to feel up to calling. It's very important," she added.

"Oh," I said, feigning compassion. "I'm sure it is. How about you tell me what you want to talk about, and I can pass on the message."

Crystal looked at Lily as if *she* might be able to talk some sense into me.

The teacup rattled on the saucer as Crystal set it on the coffee table. "It's a sensitive and private matter. And, information the senator needs to know, like yesterday."

"That changes everything, doesn't it?" I said. Lily's eyebrow ticked up. I think she'd lost track of this back and forth game I was playing with Crystal. To be honest, I didn't even know where it was going, but I was having fun keeping her off balance.

Crystal sighed and visibly relaxed. "I'm glad you understand."

"I'm wondering, Crystal, where you and the senator were yesterday morning?"

"I beg your pardon. What did you say?"

"Yesterday. Thursday. When Benny was murdered. Where were you and the senator?"

She brushed off her pants, which were already spotless. "What business is that of yours?" she asked in what I assumed was a voice meant to intimidate and put me in my place. "Much of the senator's schedule is private."

"Of course, silly me. Well, in that case, I don't think Sunny has anything to say to you. At this point," I leaned closer to Crystal, "she's keeping a low profile. I'm sure you understand."

"But she ran away when Officer Walker wanted to question her. What's she trying to hide?"

"I'm not sure what you're talking about. Sunny talked with Detective Crenshaw and Detective Winter right after the murder. She's not hiding anything." Was this considered a lie by omission? Oh well. "Tell me Crystal, what's so important that the senator sent you here to do some snooping?"

Crystal gasped. Maybe I'd gone too far.

She pulled herself tall, full of indignation. "I'm most certainly not *snooping*. If you must know, Benny was working for the senator on an important project. Gathering information. The senator needs the information he paid for before his meeting tomorrow. Since Benny can't present his findings, the senator asked *me* to read over the information and run the meeting."

Crystal's smug expression screamed loud and clear that she thought she was mighty important.

"Officer Walker didn't find any information at Benny's house and as a last resort, I want to ask Sunny if she knows where Benny's report is."

Crystal clamped her lips. Maybe she revealed more than she'd planned to, but now I knew her angle.

She tapped her long, painted fingernail against her ruby red lips. "Maybe *you* know where Benny's report is. Officer Walker said he found *you* up to no good at Sunny's house."

Now was my turn to show indignation. I stood up, sending Pip flying toward Crystal. The way she shrank away from the ten-pound terrier, you'd think a mountain lion was after her.

"Up to no good?" Crystal's comment dug deep under my skin. "Is that what he said? Well, for your information, I was picking up dry clothes for a woman who almost drowned after fleeing for her life."

I crossed my arms and stuck my nose in her face. "Maybe you can tell me what Officer Walker was doing barging into Sunny's house with his gun drawn on me and my husband. I'd say *he's* the one who was up to no good."

The whereabouts of Benny's report was unknown, and before I could calm down, I had to find out who stole it.

21

I decided that a change of tactics might soften Crystal and get her to open up. I sank onto the couch next to her. "Crystal, I think we all want the same thing, right?"

Lily's eyes bored into me. She had to be wondering where I was off to now, but she sipped her tea and settled in for the show.

"I mean... to find Benny's killer." I blew on my tea and watched Crystal from the corner of my eye.

Pip, always a friendly little hostess, must have sensed my strategy. She belly-crawled along the center cushion right up to Crystal's thigh, receiving a tentative scratch under her chin for her effort. The Pipsqueak groaned in ecstasy and scooched even closer.

Maybe I'd been wrong about Crystal after her first reaction to Pip. She must be one of those slow-to-warm-up types.

And, apparently Pip liked her, if that meant anything. I always thought she was a good judge of character, but now it seemed attention was her driving force.

"I think we got off on the wrong foot," Crystal said as she continued to work her magic on Pip. Or vice versa. I wasn't sure who had the upper hand. "I've been under a lot of stress from Senator Nash. He's getting pressured to push this project forward, but he wants to be absolutely certain it's the correct decision. Benny's research is critical. And now…"

She let that thought hang in the air. Lily and I knew what she meant—she needed that information.

"I totally get it, Crystal," I said. "You're caught in the middle taking all the heat from every which way, aren't you? I mean, you're only doing your job and trying to keep everyone happy, right?"

I made a tut-tut noise, hoping I sounded appropriately sympathetic. If I was lucky, she might share some of the pieces in this mysterious puzzle.

"I found out some interesting details on my own." I looked at her to be sure she was paying attention. Oh yeah, her ears were tuned in. "For instance," I said, "I know this important project you mentioned involves Nine Pine Nursery and turning that lovely piece of land into a golf course."

I let that settle in the room for Crystal to digest. By the scowl on her face, she wasn't taking it too well.

"Did *Hunter* tell you that? He never knows when to keep his mouth shut. Senator Nash told the five of us involved to keep a lid on this project until it was a go. At the right time he planned a big special unveiling, pulling out all the stops for the kick-off publicity campaign."

"It wasn't Hunter," I said, bursting her balloon. She bristled with irritation. "He hinted at a project, but he never said what it was." I watched Crystal's mouth form a big round circle. She'd just let the cat, plus all the toys, out of her bag.

"Well, I suppose it doesn't matter now anyway unless I can find Benny's information. Without an environmental study, the project might be doomed."

By now, Pip was curled up on Crystal's lap. *She* didn't seem to mind, but a jolt of jealousy twisted in my gut.

"Without a *positive* environmental study." I

corrected Crystals' statement. "How do you know Benny's study favors this project?"

Crystal flicked her hand like there wasn't any possibility of anything *but* a positive recommendation from Benny's impact study. She leaned forward like we were now in her inner circle, and she could share top secret information with us. "Well, Josh assured us that nothing could get in the way of the plan."

I looked at Lily. "A Josh Whiting is on the list of the dinner guests," she said.

"Josh," I let the name roll off my tongue. "What's his connection?" I asked Crystal, pretending I didn't already know his involvement from Maggie's research. She'd blabbed plenty already so why stop now?

"Really? You don't know Josh Whiting?" She almost swooned right off the cushion with her obvious admiration of the man.

I shook my head and leaned forward to give her my undivided attention. The way she whispered his name showed she revered him as if he were royalty.

"He's only the biggest, most well-known contractor in all of the Blueberry Bay area," she said. "Josh always wins the best contracts involving anything of significance. His projects are worth nothing less than a million dollars. Google his name and you'll find plenty about him."

Thank you, Maggie, for being on that already.

"Even if it means he has to resort to murder?" The words just fell out of my mouth before I could stop them. "Does this Josh Whiting own a cigarette boat by any chance?"

Crystal's hand covered her mouth, and she stood up. "I should leave."

I grabbed her arm. "You may as well spit out everything that you know about him because I'll find out anyway. And Crystal, if you try to hide even one teeny tiny morsel, it kind of makes you look guilty of something, too."

She paled.

"As Senator Nash's right-hand person, you *knew* that Benny would be out on his boat this morning taking more photos for the Senator's study, didn't you? Think about it, Crystal. Unless you have an alibi, you'll come under intense scrutiny. So, where *were* you?"

"I... ah... I... can't say.

Sue Ellen pushed through the door carrying a beautiful flower arrangement that looked very famil-iar. "There you are, Lily." She gushed as if she really hadn't had a clue where she'd find the owner of the

Blue Moon Inn. "The delivery man was at the front door when I arrived, so I said I'd bring this beauty right in for you. Isn't it gorgeous? Should we put it here on the coffee table?"

Sue Ellen flashed a wink at me that no one else could see.

The spicy aroma of snapdragons mixed with lilies and daisies wafted toward me as Sue Ellen swept passed. The arrangement had been in Lily's office when I'd arrived with Sue Ellen earlier. What she was up to? But, in the hope of finding out more from Crystal, I bit my tongue and waited.

"Oops," Sue Ellen said as a small white envelope fluttered to the floor. "Do you have a secret admirer, Lily?" Sue Ellen wiggled her eyebrows and scooped it up, slipping the card out before we could stop her."

"Sue Ellen, "I said as she held the card up to read it. "Don't be so nosy."

"Thinking of you and can't wait to see you again. H," Sue Ellen read, ignoring me.

"Oh, dear." She looked flustered, so I couldn't be sure if she was acting or if the card was real.

A rosy blush traveled up Crystal's neck straight to her cheeks.

"Oh, this must be for you, Crystal," Sue Ellen

said. "This is from *your* secret admirer. I'm so sorry," Sue Ellen handed the card to Crystal.

"We're just friends," Crystal mumbled and stuffed the card in her pocket.

"Maybe *H* is your alibi for yesterday?" I asked. "That's not Hunter Bodane by any chance, is it? I couldn't help noticing his transformation when you drove into Nine Pine Nursery yesterday. As soon as he saw you, Crystal, he couldn't wait to get away from me." I grinned. "He's certainly a handsome and friendly guy. No doubt, a good catch. And wealthy too, if the sale of his nursery goes through."

Crystal's eyes widened as she looked at the three of us staring at her. Did she feel like she'd walked into a trap?

"It's nothing like that," she stammered as she picked up her leather bag.

What was it then? But I didn't have a chance to ask her because she was out the door in three long strides.

What was she hiding?

22

*S*ue Ellen helped herself to a cookie from the tray on the coffee table.

"Scooch over a little bit, Pippy," she said as she wiggled her backside to squeeze onto Crystal's spot.

"My, my, my," I said to Sue Ellen, trying not to laugh. "I'm a little bit flabbergasted. You drove Lily's guest right out the door, which doesn't fit with your normal southern hospitality."

"Well," she said after she finished her cookie, "there was no way *Maggie* could pull off waltzing in here with a flower arrangement as a prop. *She* said because of my special brand of charm, I was the only one who could pretend that flower arrangement had just been delivered. And, if I don't say so myself, I handled it magnificently."

Maggie pushed through the door, followed by Jasper and Sunny. "Absolutely brilliant, Sue Ellen. I listened to your whole performance. You should get an award," Maggie said, high-fiving Sue Ellen.

"Another cookie will do, thank you very much." The grin on her face said it all and she rewarded herself from the tray.

Sunny sat on an ottoman. "What do we do now? It won't take Crystal long to find out that Hunter didn't send those flowers."

Maggie shrugged as if that was so inconsequential it wouldn't make any difference. "Crystal is staying here tonight, right Lily?"

"That *was* the plan. I was asked to get several rooms ready at the last minute." Lily glanced at Sunny, "Thanks for your help. Crystal called to say she needed to come early to be sure everything was ready and the way the senator wants it before he arrives. I don't know if she'll actually come back now, though."

"She'll be back." Maggie said. "Put those flowers in her room as a nice reminder that she can't steam roll over us. Dani, I loved your question about the cigarette boat. I'm thinking it probably just fell out of your mouth like happens so often with you, but it was the perfect question." Maggie paced around the room. "Guess what I discovered?"

"The boat that rammed into Fish Tales?" Sunny sat up straight with a glow on her face, excited and hopeful.

I hoped that was exactly what Maggie had discovered.

"That would be great, but unfortunately, also too easy," Maggie said.

Sunny shrank back onto the ottoman.

Maggie continued, "I did learn something interesting about Josh Whiting and his pride and joy cigarette boat. A big powerful boat that he takes out every chance he gets. And, guess what? According to the harbor master at the marina in Pineville, Josh's boat was out yesterday morning." Maggie grinned like a Cheshire cat. "So, it *could* be the boat that rammed Fish Tales, Sunny, but there's no proof. Yet."

"How'd you get that detail about his boat, Mags?" I asked, even though I had a pretty good idea of her technique.

"I'll share one of my special skills." She fluttered her eyelashes. "I had to shamelessly flirt with the harbor master to get his tongue loosened. It only took a few flutters. It's just one of the tricks in my toolbox that I save for special occasions. Please don't tell AJ about that."

The four of us jerked our heads around as one at the sound of a voice in the doorway.

"AJ! When did you get here?" I asked. With such terrible timing. Pip hadn't even bothered to jump off the couch to let us know we had company. She was really slacking on her job.

AJ stared at us, well, mostly at Maggie with pink flushing her cheeks. I'd safely bet that he'd heard all about her shameless flirting, and he wasn't too happy about it.

"Don't tell me what, Maggie?" The harshness in his words felt like a wet blanket suffocating us.

Oh boy, poor Maggie. It wasn't bad enough that AJ hated when she got involved in an investigation. Adding flirting to the equation wasn't going to help their relationship.

"Hey, AJ." Maggie said. "It wasn't *real* flirting." She sounded a bit annoyed. Maybe she'd finally found herself in this relationship and wasn't going to be the lovesick teenager anymore. I hoped, for her sake.

"There's such a thing as *fake* flirting?" he asked.

"I was only chatting with the harbor master in Pineville about Josh Whiting's boat. Did you know that he has a cigarette boat, which I believe was seen speeding out of Blueberry Bay around the time of the murder?"

"I am aware of that from talking to the harbor master myself," AJ said with a smirk on his face. "But the harbor master couldn't confirm that it was Josh Whiting in the boat at the time Benny was murdered."

Sunny jumped up. "Was it the killer on the boat?"

"Maybe," AJ said, "or, maybe not. The boat is missing. This is exactly why I don't like it when you do your amateur sleuthing. Besides putting yourselves in danger, you jump to conclusions without all the evidence."

Sue Ellen picked up the tray of goodies and approached AJ. "Bless your heart, Detective. Here. Try one of Lily's deliciously scrumptious cookies. It might put you in a better mood. We aren't the enemy, you know. I'm sure all your hard work to bring this murderer to justice puts a lot of stress and strain on you." She bumped AJ's chest with the tray. "Oops, sorry."

He licked the corner of his lips. His hand hovered over the tray. "Just one and then I have some questions for Sunny."

Sunny's gaze jumped around the room. I was worried she was about to bolt again. "Can you question Sunny here?" I asked.

He nodded affirmatively while he finished his cookie.

I stood shoulder to shoulder next to Sunny.

"But without you, Dani," AJ said. "I need to talk to her alone. Is there a private room for us, Lily?"

Sunny wrapped her hand around Jasper's neck. "Can Jasper come with me?" She asked the question, but I could tell there was only one correct answer if AJ wanted her to cooperate.

"Sure."

Sunny sighed with relief. "Okay, then. I'll talk to you. I don't have anything to hide."

"I hope not," AJ said. "Lily? Can you please show us where we can talk privately? And," he stared at me, "no listening at the door."

"*Moi*?" I said in my best totally innocent voice. "I'm insulted, AJ."

"Sure you are," he mumbled as he followed Lily, Sunny, and Jasper out of the sitting room.

As soon as the door closed, I grabbed Maggie and Sue Ellen by their arms. "I know where they'll be, and we won't have to listen at the door. Come on. He'll never know."

"Famous last words," Maggie muttered but she didn't balk when I pulled her along.

"How exciting," Sue Ellen said, rubbing her hands together. "I love this cloak and dagger stuff of yours, Dani. It gives me the most delicious chills." She actually shivered when I glanced at her.

That was one of us. Sue Ellen had no clue about the dangerous side of what we did.

Especially for Sunny and me.

he sprawling Blue Moon Inn had a cozy apartment on the first floor that Lily used for her private living quarters.

As we made our way through the inn's kitchen, Lily joined us. The gleam in her eye told me she knew exactly where I was headed.

"I'm coming, too, Dani. And I have a surprise for you, but we have to be deathly quiet." She waved us along behind her as we all tiptoed through a door into Lily's bedroom.

She put her finger to her lips and said, "Shh," then slowly opened a closet door. I heard a faint background murmur but no distinct words.

Lily worked a knot in the wood loose, setting free a whiff of pine scent and revealing a hole into the closet in Lily's office. AJ's baritone voice, muffled, but clear enough, met our ears.

"Do you understand, Sunny?" his voice boomed.

I didn't hear her answer, but I assumed she nodded. What else could she do?

"I think it's safer talking to you here." I heard AJ say. "What I want to stress," a long pause made my heart pound. I hoped he couldn't hear it through the closet. "You should *not* go anywhere by yourself. I'm worried that you are also in danger because of what the murderer might think you know. Sunny, do you know what Benny was working on?"

Sunny's tentative, trembling voice came through the knot hole. "He told me he was working on an environmental impact study for a potential golf course project at the site of Nine Pine Nursery. Beyond that, I don't know what he discovered."

"But he did have notes or something, right?"

Silence from Sunny, but she must have nodded affirmatively because AJ asked, "Where are they?"

"I don't know. Honestly. Yesterday, when Benny picked me up at my house, he left a folder on my kitchen counter. He told me that he'd pick it up when he brought me home."

"You haven't been home since Benny picked you up?"

"No. You told me not to leave Misty Harbor and I haven't," Sunny said firmly, leaving no doubt. "Dani offered to go to my house and get me a change of clothes. I asked her to find the folder and bring that back, too."

"Did she bring it back?"

"She said she couldn't find it."

"Ms. Shaw?" AJ asked. I had a sinking feeling when he dropped using her first name. "Your family, at one time, owned the Nine Pine Nursery property. Isn't that right?"

Silence, except for Sue Ellen behind me who let out a gasp. I turned to see Lily pulling her away from the closet. With only Maggie at my side now, I had room to stretch. And breathe.

Finally, Sunny's voice piped up again. "With no disrespect, Detective, I don't know what difference it makes that my family *used* to own that piece of property."

I heard a chair scrape along the floor. I looked through the knothole but only saw a bit of light coming through the cracked closet door.

"It matters because I think it puts you in danger. The way I see it, whoever killed your friend, Benny Chadman, wanted to stop him from speaking about his environmental study. There are several reasons this impacts you, Sunny. First, and most obvious, is that you were with Benny when he was murdered, which means the killer might think you can identify them."

"I was in the bathroom," Sunny protested. "I didn't see *anything*, Detective." The panic in her voice stabbed at my heart.

"*I'm* not saying you saw anything. I only want to stress that the killer might jump to that conclusion. You need to understand this possibility. Okay?"

"Okay."

"Second," AJ continued, "the killer might think Benny shared his information with you."

"But he didn't. I only knew what he was studying but not his conclusions."

"I understand that. Third, since your family used to own that property, there's a chance, maybe small, but still a possibility, that the killer might think that *you* shared Benny's opposition to the golf course project and that *you* might try to stop the project from going forward even though Benny can't stop it now."

Suddenly, I was suffocating in the closet.

I needed air.

I stepped back, landing on Maggie's foot.

She yelped.

We heard shuffling on the other side of the closet wall. "What's going on there?" AJ's angry voice shouted. "Is that you, Dani?"

"Yes. I'm here in Lily's apartment, getting something. Where are you?" I grimaced and looked at Maggie, whispering, "Will he believe that?"

"Very unlikely," Maggie said. "Too bad. He knows Sunny will tell us everything anyway. He didn't share details about the investigation, just all the warnings, which most likely has Sunny scared to death. Let's go."

"To where?"

"We're going to turn Sunny's house upside down looking for Benny's folder. Just in case it's still there. I know it's a long shot, but maybe this is our lucky day," Maggie said as she moved from Lily's apartment into the kitchen. "Anything around here to take along for lunch?"

"Where are you going?" AJ asked when we stumbled into each other back in the kitchen.

"I'm taking Sunny to her house to get some more stuff," I said before Maggie had a chance to stick her foot in her mouth.

"Good idea. If you find anything interesting," he gave me a stern look, "let me know."

AJ smiled and whispered something in Maggie's ear. She frowned.

I didn't have a clue what that was about, but she'd tell me if and when she wanted to. Now, I was more concerned about getting to Sunny's house.

"I wish I could come with you," Sue Ellen said, "but Lily asked me to help her with all the last-minute decorating details."

I suspected that was just an excuse. Even though Sue Ellen said all the cloak and dagger stuff was exciting, actually going somewhere that might be dangerous was another story.

"It shouldn't take long. Besides, if we all go, we'd be tripping over each other," I said, giving her an out.

We hopped into Maggie's Jeep and left for Pineville. Maggie and Sunny sat in the front, and I squished in the back between Pip and Jasper. I didn't mind, it gave me a chance to think about the information I had while Maggie and Sunny's conversation buzzed in the background. At this point, it seemed that Hunter and Josh had plenty to gain if the golf course went forward.

Crystal would benefit, too, for that matter from involvement in such a high-profile project. What about Senator Nash? He probably welcomed any publicity for his political career. And that left Officer Walker. He was invited to the meeting, but I couldn't see how he was tied into all this.

"Hey, Mags," I said, "What did AJ whisper in your ear back in Lily's kitchen?"

She looked at me in the rearview mirror and frowned. "He just had to rub in the fact that he knew we were eavesdropping. He said I had to improve my technique. Well, I'll show *him* who needs to improve his technique when *we* solve this case."

I was sorry I'd asked. Maggie and AJ turned everything into a competition, but today went well beyond most of their silly games and could put us right smack in the middle of a deadly situation.

Maggie parked her Jeep in front of Sunny's house. Jasper raced to the front door first with Pip on her heels.

"Good to be home, huh Jasper?" Sunny asked as she unlocked her front door. It sounded more like she was referring to herself with that comment.

We all filed inside.

Sunny gasped.

I stared.

Maggie cursed.

Sunny stared dumbfounded at the mess that filled her house. Every cushion ripped apart, every drawer dumped out, and every cupboard empty. Papers covered the floor.

With her hand covering her mouth and tears rolling down on her cheeks, she whispered, "Who did this?"

I put my arm around her shoulder. "I don't know but you have to call the police and file a report."

I could feel her tremble under my hand.

"I'll help you."

Before we could do anything, someone walked in behind us.

"Sunny! Finally, you're home." I turned to see the women who'd peered at me from behind the curtains the last time I visited Sunny's home. "I've been worried about you," she said.

The disaster around us must have registered as the woman froze in place. "What happened here?" she asked in disbelief.

Sunny turned around. "Tilly!" She rushed into the older woman's arms.

Tilly embraced Sunny, patting her back and cooing soothing noises. "Don't worry, honey. Let's get you out of here." She gently turned Sunny toward the door. "We'll all go—your friends and the dogs— to my house, so we can talk. I'll help you any way I can. Come on."

I had to assume that someone out there thought Sunny knew *something*, most likely connected to Benny's environmental study. Whatever that knowledge was, it threatened their plans.

AJ was right to be concerned for Sunny's safety.

Outside, I scanned the street. It was one of those surreal moments when you know with absolute certainty that something was very wrong, but the world seemed as normal as ever with blue sky overhead, birds chirping in the trees, and a cooling breeze ruffling my curls.

Definitely weird.

What was going on?

*a*fter Sunny reported the break-in to the Pineville police, we all followed Tilly across the street.

Tilly's orderly ranch house was a welcome sight after the ransacked mess of Sunny's home. "Make yourselves comfortable," she said, waving us into the living room, "while I get some lemonade."

Maggie's stomach growled so loudly I had to laugh. In the year or so that I'd known her, she was always hungry. I chalked it up to the fact that she didn't cook and relied on the rest of us to provide handouts. Sort of like feeding a stray cat.

"I'll rustle up some crackers, too, if I can find any, but don't expect anything fancy. I don't cook," Tilly added. I chuckled again at how much Tilly reminded me of Maggie even with at least thirty or forty years separating them.

Nothing about Tilly or her modest surroundings conveyed fancy, but the woman Sunny described as her 'pistol-packing guardian grannie', came through loud and clear as strong, independent, and tough as nails. I breathed a sigh of relief knowing she was on Sunny's side.

As I wondered where we'd all sit, a large ginger cat sauntered in and plopped down exactly in the middle of the living room. Owning it with a glare at us. Pip approached but the cat quickly warned her away with a loud hiss and swipe.

Poor Pip.

"Pinky, play nice," Sunny said. "Pip won't hurt you."

I had to agree, but I couldn't say the same for Tilly's cat. Even with a name like Pinky, carrying twice Pip's weight and needle-sharp claws, I was positive she'd hand out some serious damage if given the opportunity.

Tilly returned carrying a tray with glasses, a pitcher, and a box of crackers. "Here we go."

Sunny took over the serving duty while Tilly scooped up Pinky and sat in a low wooden rocker. The cat curled in her lap but kept gazing at all of us.

In her mind, I could tell she had no doubt who belonged here and who didn't. She planned to keep order no matter what.

Jasper sprawled in the middle of the room, about the only spot with enough space for her. Pip, giving up on befriending Pinkie, jumped on the couch and claimed the cushion between Maggie and myself. After we all had lemonade, Sunny pulled a chair next to Tilly's, angling it so she had a view of her house across the street. By the looks of it, she didn't plan to miss anyone passing through or stopping by for a visit.

An SUV with blue lights flashing on top pulled to a stop outside her house. Sunny visibly stiffened when Officer Walker stepped out of the police car.

"I'll go over there with you, Sunny," I said. I stood up and waited at the door with Pip. I had no intention of leaving her alone with someone she distrusted and feared. Apparently Jasper planned to be part of the guard team, too. Good.

As soon as we were out of earshot, I asked, "What is it about Mick Walker that makes you so scared of him?"

Sunny looked at me with a steely expression in her eyes. "He let the power of his police position turn him into a first-class bully." She spit out each word. "He pushes the limit of what he *should* be doing to protect Pineville to include how he can help himself."

"Do you know how he's involved in this golf course project?" I asked. "He's on the list for the meeting at the Blue Moon Inn."

"I'm not sure, but I think he's finagling for some kind of financial benefit. He could be an investor, although I don't think he has that kind of money at this point in his life. More likely, he's hoping for a cushy, well-paid position as a security consultant or something like that."

"He'd give up his current job for that?"

"I've heard that his current job isn't very secure," Sunny said. "If that's true, he'd team up with anyone if he thought they'd be able to help him down the line."

We walked slowly toward Officer Walker who leaned against his car as if he didn't have a care in the world or a ransacked house to investigate.

"One more question, Sunny. How did Benny and Mick get along?"

She jerked her head around to face me. "Benny was honorable, honest, and hardworking to a fault as far as some people were concerned. He and Mick couldn't have been more different. I don't think Mick liked facing that contrast. Benny's example exaggerated his own tainted morals. It's probably safe to say that Mick hated him with a passion."

"Enough to *kill* him?" I asked, barely above a whisper.

Sunny didn't answer immediately. When we were only a half dozen steps away from Mick, she kept her eye on him, but whispered back, "Yes. If he had the chance and thought he could get away with it, I think he would. *I* always watch my back around him. Just in case."

"Hey, Sunny," Mick said, ending our conversation. He gave her a smile that made my skin crawl, but thankfully he totally ignored me. I stepped closer to Sunny making sure Mick understood I was sticking with her no matter what. "You called for help? What's going on?"

"Have you looked in my house?" she asked with disgust.

Good question. We'd seen him arrive. Why hadn't he gone in?

I stepped in front of Sunny. "Is this how you answer a call for help?" I stared at Officer Walker. I knew I was about to get under his skin.

He pushed himself off his car, lowered his arms to his side and fingered his holster. I stepped in closer, not wanting him to think he could intimidate me with his macho power trip.

"Sunny's house was ransacked. Completely torn apart," I added in case he didn't know the definition of ransacked. "It doesn't look particularly professional to casually wait out here and ogle my friend when there's a crime to investigate."

Sunny jabbed my side with her elbow, but I was on a roll. It was high time this cop learned that he worked for the people of Pineville and not the other way around. I saw Misty Harbor's police in a whole new light.

He glanced at Sunny's house. "Was anything taken?" Mick asked, trying for a commanding tone.

"It's impossible to tell, considering the mess inside. Plus, I didn't take the time to check. I didn't want to contaminate any evidence," Sunny said.

Never mind that she was scared out of her wits and wanted to just get away as quickly as possible. I was glad that she'd overcome that fear now.

Mick glared at me, but for whatever reason, he remained silent. He was probably the kind of man who'd get even when he thought I was least expecting it, but I didn't plan to linger around town long enough for that to happen.

"Follow me inside, Sunny, and we'll look around together."

Sunny latched on to my arm like a vice, dragging me along whether Officer Walker liked it or not. My best guess was that he'd be happy if the sidewalk opened up and swallowed me whole, leaving Sunny alone to deal with him. I had no intention of letting her go inside with this police officer known for his questionable scruples.

"Do you think this is connected to Benny's murder?" he asked as he led us to Sunny's front door.

"How should I know?"

"Senator Nash told me there's information floating around somewhere, and he needs to get his hands on it before tomorrow's meeting," Mick said as we stopped at Sunny's front door.

Sunny grabbed Mick's arm, forcing him to turn around. "And if he doesn't get it?"

"I don't know." Mick sounded sincere. "It's my job to help him find what he paid for and that's what I intend to do, so if you know anything—"

"If you don't find the information, the project will be canceled?" Sunny didn't let go of Mick's arm.

Her urgency about this had me wondering if she had any involvement as to why the folder had gone missing. Was I just a pawn in this whole murder investigation, running around looking in one direction when all along the evidence was somewhere else?

I didn't like the idea that I was being used, but I was in too deep to back out now.

Mick turned the doorknob. "Let's take a look inside."

25

We entered Sunny's house behind Officer Walker, along with a breeze that rustled the mess of papers on the floor. A drip, drip, drip from a leaking faucet echoed somewhere in the house, adding to the eeriness shivering through me.

I thought I'd be prepared for the disarray. I wasn't. The ripped cushions and knocked over chairs were far worse than I remembered. Whoever had done this had a purpose.

Mick turned and held his finger to his lips. "You wait here by the door while I check the rest of the downstairs."

I held a squirming Pip in my arms, but Jasper sat

calmly at Sunny's side as Mick disappeared down a hallway.

"He seemed almost too casual when we were outside, but now he's doing his job," I whispered to Sunny.

She shrugged as if to say she couldn't care less what he did. "He can do his search if that makes him feel better, but he won't find anyone in there."

"How do you know?"

Sunny's hand rested on Jasper's head. "She'd be going crazy."

I hoped Sunny was right.

Mick called out, "All's clear down here." With his gun drawn, he headed for the stairs. He returned a few minutes later and gave us the thumbs up. "You can stack up all the papers if you want to." He'd holstered his weapon. "Either someone hates you, Sunny, or they were looking for something. Are you sure Benny didn't leave any of his notes here?"

"Why would he have done that?" It didn't escape me that her reply didn't answer Mick's question.

Mick lifted his hat and ran his fingers through his thick mop of sun-bleached hair. "Well, you and Benny were thick as thieves. It seems logical to assume he might have entrusted you with something he thought was important. You know, Sunny, if he did share something with you, it could put you in danger, too."

He stared at Sunny for another minute before he shook his head as if there were something else he was about to ask but changed his mind. "I'm going to take a look outside."

"I still don't trust him," Sunny said, after he'd disappeared. She swiveled around to look at me. "Did you get the impression that his focus is only on Benny's information? For all I know, Mick is the person who tore my house apart looking for it."

"He's a police officer. You really think he'd do that?"

Sunny leaned over and scooped papers on the floor into a pile. "I might as well start cleaning up this mess," she mumbled. In her crouched position, she crab-walked, scooping and straightening until the floor was cleared. Next, she threw pillows on the couch. "Well, that's a bit better."

"You didn't answer my question, Sunny." I couldn't decide if she had ignored me or was lost in her thoughts. She'd made a serious charge.

Finally, Sunny looked at me. "We only met yesterday. You don't know much about me, Benny, Mick Walker, or any of the other people involved in this murder. Do I think Mick would tear my house apart looking for Benny's information?" She wobbled her hand back and forth. "Maybe. Maybe not. Any one of the people invited to the senator's meeting might have done it. The real question is what was so important in those papers that got my friend murdered. She spread her arm to take in the destruction of the room. "And why would someone do this? Can you answer that?"

Of course I couldn't, but before I had a chance to say anything, Mick clomped back inside.

"No obvious disturbance outside, Sunny. My advice? Stay somewhere else until this murder is solved. You don't want to make yourself an easy target. Understand?"

"Don't worry about me," Sunny said. I recognized the snippy tone of someone who didn't like to be told what to do. "Mick?"

He waited.

"Why are you so interested in Benny's research? What's in this golf course project for *you*?"

His jaw muscles clenched. Clearly, Sunny blindsided him with that question.

"I mean," she continued, "you never made it a secret that you and Benny didn't agree on developing the Nine Pine Nursery property. Now, he's dead. Out of the way. The golf course project will probably move forward, ruining that beautiful piece of oceanfront property. I think it's a fair question to ask how *you* will benefit."

I watched with fascination as these two stared at each other, locked in some kind of power trip. My money was squarely on Sunny. She'd gotten under Mick's skin when she implied that he'd benefit from Benny's murder.

His fist clenched as he struggled to maintain his control.

"I never made it a secret that I've been for the golf course right from the start. I see it as a plus for Pineville. It'll bring in tourists who'll stay in town and spend money. That's progress and a win for local businesses." He cocked his head and one eyebrow ticked up slightly. "It's obvious that you and pretty much everyone else have jumped to the conclusion that there was only one outcome of Benny's research—a negative environmental impact, stopping the golf course project." Now, Mick leaned over so his face was close to Sunny's. "What if," his pause held my attention, "Benny's research gave it a green light instead?"

Okay. I hadn't seen that coming, but Mick had a good point.

Sunny shoved him, her hands smacking against

his chest. "Are you saying that you think *I* killed Benny to stop a positive report?"

Mick grabbed her hands. Jasper growled and push between them. Mick stepped back, scowling. "I like you, Sunny. I'll ignore your assault on a police officer because I know you've been through a stressful ordeal. But I also know how you feel about that property. It used to be in your family, and you can't stand the idea of change coming. What I'm saying, loud and clear is that you, out of everyone connected to this project, would have the strongest motive to destroy Benny's work... if his conclusion *didn't* stop the golf course."

Mick glanced at me as if he wanted to be sure I'd been paying attention.

"Get. Out. Of. My. House." Sunny threw her words at Mick with such force I expected them to pierce his chest.

On his way out, he said, "That project will move forward without evidence of any negative impact on Blueberry Bay. The senator didn't need Benny's report to make a final recommendation. He thought it was the right thing to do for complete transparency and all that kind of stuff. I'll send someone over to do a thorough search for clues about the break-in."

Sunny sank onto her chair after Mick slammed the door closed. "At least I don't have to worry about him bothering me anymore," she said. "That's one good thing."

Yeah, that was one way to look at it, but I had to consider what he'd said. Did Sunny send me on a wild goose chase for a folder that either never existed or that she'd already destroyed?

I considered the possibility that Benny showed her his findings while they were on his boat. Findings that indicated the golf course would not impact Blueberry Bay. Did they argue, only to have it end in a terrible tragedy? Then, Sunny jumped overboard, fleeing the scene of the crime after throwing the report into the ocean.

Completely possible.

I shuddered at that scenario.

I scratched between Pip's ears. If only she could talk to Jasper and tell me what *really* happened on Fish Tales when Benny was murdered. Wouldn't that make life so much simpler?

Now, this new angle festered like a big infected splinter as I wondered if Sunny was hiding a secret.

26

I left a dejected Sunny sitting in her house with only Jasper to comfort her while I walked back to Tilly's house. In my opinion, a few minutes alone to process Mick's accusation would do her good.

Besides, I wanted time to let Maggie know what had happened.

A welcome but unexpected sound of laughter greeted my ears. Tilly had Maggie in stitches over one of her stories, but they both wiped their grins off their faces as soon as they saw me.

"Don't you look like something Pinky dragged in during a wild and windy night," Tilly said. I self-consciously ran my fingers through my tangled curls, knowing it wouldn't make much difference.

"What happened?" Maggie asked. "And *please* don't tell me that you left Sunny alone with Officer Walker."

"Sunny's alone with Jasper, and we need to get her out of her house. Out of town, Mags. Officer Walker is sending someone back to look for clues about the break-in, and for her own safety, we need to convince her to leave until this murder is solved. Both Detective Crenshaw and Officer Walker told her she might be a target now."

Tilly stood up and jammed her hands on her hips. "Sunny knows she and Jasper can stay here with me. I'll keep her safe. The last thing she should do is let Mick run her out of town."

Pinky's tail fuzzed out like a bottle brush. Did she have her hackles up at the news she'd have to share her house with a giant Newfoundland?

I quickly formulated a plan. "Here's what I think," I said. "Tilly, you have the perfect vantage point to keep an eye on Sunny's house in case anyone comes snooping around again. If she's gone, they might feel more emboldened to do just that. We'll keep her safe with my friend at the Blue Moon Inn."

Maggie nodded enthusiastically.

From the scowl on Tilly's face, I could tell she

wasn't having my plan. "I see a big problem, Dani. "How will you convince Sunny to leave? She doesn't like anyone to tell her what to do. Nope. As a matter of fact, for as long as I've known her, she'll do just the opposite. She'll dig her heels in and invite danger to her doorstep."

I grinned, anticipating this problem. "If she stays at the inn, she's right in the middle of the action. Senator Nash is supposed to arrive tonight for a brunch meeting tomorrow about the pros and cons of turning the Nine Pine Nursery into a golf course. At least, I think the meeting is still a go. Sunny can stay in the background and listen to what's going on. I think that will tempt her."

"Eavesdrop?" Tilly asked, showing a smirk of satisfaction. "Who will be there besides the senator?"

I looked at Maggie. "Do you have the list?"

"Sure do." She tapped the side of her head. "It's all up here—Senator Nash, his assistant, Crystal Wilson, Hunter Bodane, the owner of Nine Pine Nursery, your friendly police officer, Mick Walker, and the contractor, Josh Whiting. I'm following an interesting tidbit about Mr. Whiting."

"I know that sleazy operator," Tilly said with disgust lacing her words. "He buys low, treats his subcontractors like dirt, and manages to cheat them out of their money, and then gets top dollar for whatever he builds. I've always wondered who he has on his payroll doing some bullying behind the scene."

"You mean someone like Officer Walker?" Maggie asked taking the words right out of my mouth. "He seems like someone who'd fit that bill and that's the lead I've been following."

"I've always wondered about that, too," Tilly said. "Somehow, nothing illegal has tarnished him, but one of these days he'll get his due."

"He seems to know how to stay within the legal lines. I heard from my detective friend." Maggie glanced at me but didn't name a name. It had to be AJ. "He said that Mick is angling for a favor in exchange for his help moving the golf course project swiftly and smoothly through any town hurdles. Don't ask me how I got it, but that's the latest info."

Pip jumped off my lap and dashed to the door.

Tilly pulled open a drawer in a small table next to her chair. A gun gleamed inside. She meant business.

As soon as the door opened, Jasper pranced in, tail wagging and with what looked like a smile for Pip.

Pinky, her orange fur standing on end, turned into a giant ball resembling a large pumpkin with a twitchy tail. The dogs ignored her and her hissing.

Sunny followed with a backpack slung over her shoulder. "The police came back. Without Mick," she added. "I grabbed some clothes and left. It's too depressing in there with all the mess." She looked at me. "Do you think Lily will let me stay at the inn for a few more nights?"

A quick glance at Tilly as she gave me a wink before she slammed the drawer closed, letting me know the problem was solved.

"With the way you made all the windows sparkle?" I said to Sunny. "Lily will be thrilled to have an extra pair of hands on board before the guests arrive. I can drop you off now, if that works."

"And, don't worry about a thing around here, Sunny," Tilly said. "I'll keep an eye on your place and make sure those police do their job." With a nod toward Sunny's house and raised eyebrows for emphasis, she let us all know she had everything under control at this end.

I didn't doubt her abilities. She sat in a straight-backed chair next to her little table with a fancy camera on top and her gun in the drawer. There was more to Tilly Morris than met my eyes. I wondered what lurked below the surface.

Maggie drove us to the Blue Moon Inn, making small talk with Sunny. "Your friend Tilly sure has led an interesting life."

My ears perked up.

"Did she tell you that she was the photographer for an overseas journalist? She's traveled all over the world, seen all kinds of interesting places, and speaks several languages," Sunny said. "She's got more stories than would fit in Blueberry Bay."

Maggie nodded. "She shared a couple of adventures that almost made me wet my pants I was laughing so hard."

I appreciated Maggie's effort to distract us during the ride back to Misty Harbor. Taking our minds off of Benny's murder, even if it was for only fifteen or twenty minutes, helped to clear away some of the confusing cobwebs.

I opened the front door of the Blue Moon Inn expecting the familiar background flute music and Lily's delicious cooking aromas. What I *didn't* expect was Luke's deep voice, although it made me smile at this pleasant surprise. Another familiar voice responded to Luke, but I couldn't immediately place it.

"Let *me* tell Dani, okay?" I heard Luke say as I entered the sitting room and saw that he was talking to his pilot friend, Ace Osborn.

I didn't like the sound of this. Why was Ace here with Luke?

"Tell me what?" Did I want to know?

Probably not.

Luke spun around, looking distressed. "You haven't heard yet?"

I looked at Maggie wondering if she'd forgotten to share something important with me.

She raised her shoulders, just as confused as I was.

"Sunny? Did the police in Pineville tell you something you forgot to share?" I heard the accusatory tone in my question, but right now, I was worried that maybe the police found Benny's report giving a green light for the golf course project. Sunny would hate that outcome.

She shook her head.

I looked back at Luke. "Why is Ace here?" This didn't make sense.

"He came over to tell us that while he was flying over Blueberry Bay, he saw a boat," Luke said.

"A cigarette boat." Ace added that important detail.

"Crashed on a rocky stretch of the shoreline." Ace's grim expression told me all I needed to know.

Unconsciously, my hand flew to cover my mouth and stifle a gasp. "Josh Whiting?" I asked but already knew the answer would be yes.

Luke nodded, confirming my guess. "Dead."

"An accident?" I feared the answer.

Luke shook his head with a grim look on his face. "The police haven't said yet."

27

*L*uke led me to a chair. Maggie and Sunny sat down too, like we were all waiting for an announcement that might take days to come.

Two people dead now. All because of a golf course?

Pip licked my chin, helping me focus on the here and now.

"The thing is," Ace said. We all looked at him hoping he'd have some tidbit to share about this terrible situation.

"What exactly did you see?" Maggie asked. Leave it to her to interrupt and zero in straight to the heart of the matter.

"What I was about to say is that Josh Whiting

was a boating expert. He probably spent as much time on his boat as he did on land. He knew boats and he knew the coastline." Ace rubbed his hands along his jeans as if he was drying sweaty palms. "I'm well aware, as a helicopter pilot, that something can go wrong quickly and turn an ordinary trip deadly. But you never take unnecessary risks. It doesn't make sense to me that Josh would have gone dangerously close to shore in that area. It's known for tricky currents and hidden rocks. It's possible his boat had a problem which forced him there. Or—"

"*You* don't think it was an accident." Maggie didn't ask Ace his opinion, she stated it.

Ace ran his hand over the stubble on his chin, carefully considering his answer. "No, I don't. And another thing that could mean something or could be a coincidence—Senator Nash's assistant was with me. She insisted that we take the flight course that took us over that spot. I can't help but wonder if she knew the boat was there and wanted me to discover it. The way it was wedged into the rocks, it would have been barely visible except from the air."

"Did she spot the boat or did you?" I asked.

"I did. She was busy reading through some papers, and in her defense, the route we took was the shortest path to her destination. I don't think she even noticed the wreckage, and I didn't point it out to her," Ace said. "It wasn't the way I wanted to go, though. I wanted to do the approach from the opposite side of the landing spot.

"Just out of curiosity, why was she with you and where was her destination?" Maggie asked.

I knew her investigative wheels were spinning behind that seemingly innocent question.

"She chartered a flight to Senator Nash's estate. He has a helipad on his property. I picked him up and flew the two of them to the hospital where he was doing some kind of ribbon cutting ceremony for a new wing or something like that. I didn't get all the details but I do know they were running late, which is probably why she didn't just drive. The senator chewed Crystal out for being late so she would have had a perfectly good reason to insist on the flight path that we took."

"Huh," I said, feeling kind of blown away at the excess of some people. "How does all this fit together?"

Sunny sat forward on the couch and said, "It could be a simple explanation. Maybe Josh was worried what Benny's report would say so he killed him before the senator's big meeting. Then, someone killed Josh to make room for a different project for that property. It sounds logical to me."

"Does logic have anything to do with murder?" I asked, shaking my head at this tragic situation. "Two people are dead."

"Or, someone double-crossed him?" Sunny's answer sounded like she was grasping at straws. "Look at who was invited to that meeting. Everyone, except Benny, wanted the golf course project to move forward."

"And you," I said.

"What?"

"*You're* against the golf course, too."

"So what? I'm not part of the group. I had no impact." She crossed her arms and glared at me.

"How do you know that everyone wanted the project to move forward?" I asked her.

"Well, Benny told me." Sunny looked around the room like she wasn't thrilled being the center of attention. She let out a deep sigh.

"Josh Whiting wouldn't jump into a project like that if he wasn't going to get a big payout. Hunter Bodane's nursery is so far underwater that his best solution is to sell to the highest bidder—Josh Whiting. I'm making an assumption about Senator Nash, but I think a big project like this would give him a lot of exposure. Good exposure. And, keep his popularity right at the top of the charts. Same with Crystal. If the senator is getting positive exposure, it reflects well on her and her ambitions to move up the ladder. Officer Mick Walker is always ready to jump on a project if it looks like he can make some money. He'll tag along any way possible. They all benefit from the project moving forward."

"Would Benny submit a phony report to stop the project?" Maggie asked. "For example, would he say the golf course would have a *negative* impact on Blueberry Bay if he didn't actually find *evidence* to support that?"

"No. Absolutely not!" Sunny said. "Benny was too honest. Everyone knew that."

"So," I said, "according to your simple explanation, Benny's report would *have* to be negative for someone to kill him in order to stop the project. There are plenty of people in that camp but..." this was the tricky angle. "If his report was *positive*, in other words, the golf course had *no negative impact*..." I paused to let that sink in, "... then *all* of those people would be clamoring to expose it; not destroy the report *or* Benny."

"Right," Sunny said with a shrug of her shoulders. "His report had to be negative."

I wasn't buying it, but I decided to leave it at that for now.

Ace checked his watch, stood up, and stretched. "I'm just the messenger so I'll leave this problem for you to hash out a solution. Now, I've got to get back to my car. Luke, can you give me a ride?"

Luke nodded. I walked with them outside to his truck.

"What do you think about Benny's report?" I asked them. I couldn't just dismiss the possibility that Benny was about to put out a positive report that *wouldn't* stop the project. If that was true, Sunny looked guilty of destroying it.

"I see where you're going," Luke said, "but do you think Sunny would have killed Benny if the report didn't stop the golf course?"

"No. I don't think she killed her friend. What I do think is very possible is that Benny, because of his friendship with Sunny, gave her a heads up that his report *wouldn't* stop the golf course. She freaked out, threw it overboard, and then locked herself in the boat's cabin. The rest of her story fits in after that scenario. Also, if she *did* kill Benny, she wouldn't have waited in my office at the Little Dog Diner for me to arrive and help her. One other point that has me baffled is that Benny told Sunny to find me if anything happened to him. Why would he do that unless he suspected foul play, which implies his report *would* be controversial? In that case, my theory flies right out the window."

"You know, Dani," Luke said as he put his arm around my shoulder. "Maybe Benny didn't tell her to find you. You have a reputation in Blueberry Bay for getting involved in solving murders. Sunny might have said that to throw everyone off from considering that Benny's report was favorable for the golf course. Maybe she found you on her own, not knowing what else to do when she swam to Misty Harbor."

Ace nodded in agreement. "Luke is right, Dani."

I was stunned that I hadn't considered such an obvious possibility. "Is it reasonable to think that Sunny is the only one who knows what was in Benny's report?"

"Of course, that's possible, more than possible considering all the interest in finding the report," Luke said like his answer was a no brainer.

Great, I thought. I had to handle Sunny with kid gloves to see if I could get her to open up and at the same time, keep her safe.

I worried that there was a real possibility that another body could turn up.

28

"Wait, Dani!"

I'd almost made it back inside the Blue Moon Inn. Almost, but not quite when AJ called out to me.

"Is there someplace we can talk?" he asked. "Privately?"

I led him to the side entrance that took us into Lily's apartment. It was private enough as far as I was concerned.

"What's up?" I asked him as soon as I'd closed the door behind us.

"There's been another murder," he said. "Did you know?"

"Luke just told me there was a death, maybe an accident?" I asked hoping against hope.

"Yeah, well, it's hard to call it an accident when Josh Whiting was found shot in the head."

My gut clenched. Not because Josh was a friend. I'd never even met him. But the idea of a cold-blooded killing of anyone was enough to make me feel sick. And scared.

"Who is doing this, AJ? This, on top of someone ransacking Sunny's house. Did you know that? Will she be next?"

AJ leaned against Lily's dresser, resting his chin on the palm of his hand. "No, I didn't know, but I did tell you that I thought she could be in danger. Where is she now?"

"Here. Sunny will stay right here with Lily for at least a few days and her neighbor is keeping an eye on her house in case anyone comes back. Officer Walker was the responding officer when she called it in. It was weird. He kept asking her if she had any information from Benny, like he assumed that was the only reason for anyone to break-in to her house. He seemed to be obsessed about Benny's report related to the golf course project."

I couldn't read AJ's expression until his jaw muscles clenched, letting me know he didn't like what I'd just told him.

A squeaky door from the kitchen leading into

Lily's apartment distracted both of us. Were we talking too loudly, attracting unwanted company?

Pip squeezed through, looked at the both of us, and wagged her stubby tail like she'd just found the hidden prize and expected a reward.

I bent down and clapped my hands together. "Pippy! Have you been looking for me? Did Jasper tell you something interesting?"

"Huh?" AJ's eyebrows knitted together. "Are you kidding me? Pip is telling you details now from Sunny's big dog?"

I chuckled and watched a pink flush of embarrassment color AJ's cheeks. I guessed he hadn't meant to let that thought slip out. "I ask her, but so far she hasn't shared anything." I teased. "But, don't worry, I'll keep trying. What do I have to lose?"

"Only someone thinking you've lost your marbles," AJ mumbled, but the edge of his lips twitched. Everyone who knew me had heard me talking to Pip, so that in itself wasn't strange. I guess the fact that I hoped for an answer was going a bit too far for them. What they didn't understand was that dogs communicated in many ways, and I didn't expect Pip to actually speak *words* to me. The real benefit of talking to Pip was how it helped me work through situations. It helped a lot. And she had an uncanny way of making me understand her side of our unconventional conversations.

Pip pawed at my leg. "See?" I said to AJ. "She's telling me it's time to leave Lily's room. Something is happening that she wants me to know about."

He chuckled a little nervously. "Sure. You got all that from a scratch on your leg?" His skepticism obvious. "She probably just wants you to pick her up."

"That too." I scooped my little sidekick into my arms. "Let's go, Pipster. Lead the way. AJ? You can come too... or sneak out unseen the way we came in."

He hesitated.

I knew I'd tickled his curiosity about the unknown beyond Lily's apartment door. Even if it turned out to be nothing. AJ would get great satisfaction from proving I was a little bit wacky if Pip's scratch did turn out to mean that she only wanted me to pick her up. I walked out with her in my arms, and AJ did follow us.

The delicious aromas in Lily's kitchen practically knocked me over. With my eyes closed, I inhaled deeply, savoring the scent of her seafood casserole and fresh garlic bread.

My taste buds begged for a sample.

"Dani? AJ? Where'd the two of you come from?" Lily asked, patting her chest and catching her breath after the initial shock of seeing us appear as if out of thin air.

I leaned against the counter and sighed before sharing the news. "AJ just told me about Josh Whiting. His boat crashed." I hungrily eyed the platter of stuffed mushrooms cooling on the counter.

The pan in Lily's hand crashed onto the counter. "Is he alright?"

I shook my head. "I should have phrased that differently. He was murdered. I don't know which came first, the gunshot to his head or his boat crashing. AJ?"

"No comment on that."

Color drained from Lily's face as I gave her the details. "That's terrible," she said softly, still in shock. Then she looked at us. "At this rate, no one will be left to come to the senator's brunch tomorrow. What the heck is going on around here?" Lily stared at AJ waiting for an answer to a question that didn't have one. Yet. She sighed and pointed to the door leading out of the kitchen. "Maggie's in the sitting room with the senator and Crystal. Do they know about this yet?"

"I don't know. I'll go out and talk to them," AJ

said. He walked away slowly with his shoulders slumped. It had to be a conversation he was dreading.

I elbowed him as he walked past me. "Pip's one clever canine, right?"

AJ ignored my comment. He didn't appreciate my attempt to lighten his mood. Oh well.

"Pip's right about what?" Lily asked.

"She found me in your apartment and let me know something was going on out here. AJ didn't believe there was anything to Pip's scratch on my leg. He was wrong. Right, Pipster?" I reached into Lily's jar of homemade dog treats for a reward. "Here you go," I said to the miniature marvel.

"Where's Sunny?" I asked Lily while Pip enjoyed her peanut butter treat. "Do you have her busy somewhere out of the way?" At this point, I didn't think it would do Sunny any good to be confronted by yet another person looking for Benny's report.

Lily slid hot mini quiches onto a cooling rack. The food surrounding me, from these steaming mini quiches to the stuffed mushrooms, were impossible to resist.

"They're for the guests, Dani," Lily said as she slapped my hand away from one of the hot little cups of egg and cheese.

"Sunny took Jasper out for a walk. And, as much help as she's been here, I really can't have them around tonight or during tomorrow's brunch." Lily put a dirty pan in the sink. "Sunny can stay, but I don't think she will without Jasper. You know, not everyone is a fan of a big slobbery dog. My priority is to make a great impression and hope for more recommendations."

"I'll talk to Luke and see if he minds if Sunny and Jasper stay with us at Sea Breeze. I feel like I've barely been home for the last couple of days. I'll find Sunny and let her know."

"Or, ask Rose. She called here earlier wondering where you've been. She's worried about you, Dani. You know she's always willing to help."

Of course my grandmother would worry, but she also knew I had to do what I had to do. She'd never tell me to stop searching for answers. Only to be careful. After all, I'd gotten this insatiable curiosity for truth from her.

"And don't forget about the chowder you promised to make for the brunch tomorrow." Lily wiped her hands on her apron. "Are you sure you'll have time, or should I figure something else out?" She eyed me suspiciously, knowing that I had forgotten but was kind enough to give me an out.

I almost smacked the side of my head but that would have admitted to Lily that I did, in fact, forget. Instead, I nodded. "I'll make it tonight. Don't worry." She'd helped Sunny when I asked. I couldn't let her down now after I'd made a promise. Good thing she reminded me though, I thought guiltily. Was this murder consuming too much of my time?

"No!"

A desperate shriek pierced through the Blue Moon Inn making the hair on my neck stand on end.

I looked at Lily. "Who is that?"

"It must be Crystal." Lily said as she untied her apron, threw it on the counter, and made a beeline toward her guests.

I followed. All thoughts of finding Sunny and heading home to relax... gone... for the moment.

29

*I*t only took seconds to assess the situation in Lily's sitting room.

Crystal, with her head in her hands, sobbed while Senator Nash patted her back. AJ, having just shared the news of Josh Whiting's murder, paced in front of the coffee table. Apparently, a crying woman, left him at a loss for what to do.

Lily crouched in front of Crystal offering sympathetic condolences, while AJ maneuvered me out of the room.

"Where's Maggie?" he whispered. "She told me she'd be here with the senator, and I don't see hide nor hair of her. And, where's Sunny? You said she was here, too," AJ demanded. "Something strange is going on and that's usually when I know you're up to something, Dani."

"Slow down." I whispered back. "I walked in when you did, AJ." I tried to control my annoyance, but it wasn't working. "Lily said that Sunny took Jasper for a walk. I'm sure she'll be right back. Where can she go? As far as *I* know, she doesn't know anyone in town. I don't know where Maggie is, maybe in the powder room?"

As we talked, I heard the front door open and a rush of nails clicked on the wood floor straight toward the sitting room.

Before I could block the doorway, Jasper pushed by me and filled the room with her massive size and a roar of barks.

Crystal jumped onto the couch.

The senator froze.

I grabbed Jasper's collar and yanked her one hundred plus pounds with all my strength. Bit by bit I managed to force her out of the room. Behind me, Lily's calm voice soothed her guests. I didn't dare look at her. This was exactly what she'd been worried about. I owed her a lot more than chowder after this invasion. Jasper had to leave.

"Where the heck is Sunny?" I asked Maggie after

I got the big dog outside with a little encouragement from Pip. "They're always together."

"I have to talk to AJ, and then I'll tell you what happened," Maggie said as she headed back inside.

"Wait!" I grabbed her arm. "Is Sunny alright?"

"For now. I'll be right back. I had to make a quick decision, and I hope it works out like I planned." Maggie disappeared inside leaving me with a very upset dog and a mind swirling with questions. What decision? I wondered.

I stroked the soft fur on Jasper's head, which helped to settle her down. It calmed me, too. Together, we sat on the front step. I kept a tight grip on her leash.

"What's going on?" I wrapped my arm around her. Jasper looked at me with her sensitive brown eyes. Pip added her sympathetic expression, too. "You know something isn't right, don't you?" Jasper's tail swished behind us, stirring up a cloud of dust.

Before my one-sided conversation got any further, the door opened and closed behind us.

"Let's get out of here. Quick," Maggie said. She put her hand on my shoulder and jumped over the granite step on her way toward her Jeep.

I followed since it was my only option if I wanted to find out what happened to Sunny and why Jasper was here without her. From the front passenger seat, I glanced at the inn and sent a silent message to Lily that I'd be back as soon as possible.

"Don't worry. Lily knows what happened."

"You can read minds now?" I asked.

"Uh... no. You just said sorry to Lily."

Of course I did. Me and that habit of letting my thoughts escape through my mouth. "So, Mags, what's all this cloak and dagger stuff that you've got going on?"

Maggie turned onto Main Street, squealing her tires just a little in her race to get away from the inn. "Oops," she said and looked in the rearview mirror. "It doesn't look like anyone is following us."

I swiveled my head around, wondering who she thought would bother to follow us, but Jasper's big head blocked my view. "Is it because we have Jasper with us? Someone is after *her*?" I tried to make sense of something.

Maggie took a couple of quick turns down side streets and followed a road parallel to Main. She checked the rearview mirror again and finally slowed down, letting out a deep sigh. "There, I think we're safe now."

"Safe from *what*?" I asked, thoroughly confused by her evasive driving maneuver. "Should I be worried about something?"

"I took Sunny to your house. She was about to walk straight into the arms of Crystal and Senator Nash so I snuck outside and convinced her she needed to go with me."

I glanced back at the enormous dog. "Why didn't you leave Jasper with her?"

"That's the brilliant part of my plan, Dani. When I went inside, I told AJ that I found Jasper wandering on Main Street. Alone. Dragging her leash. I told him I didn't know what happened to Sunny. Of course, I managed to get Lily out of the room and told her the truth. She'll tell AJ as soon as he gets away from the senator."

"Why the deception?"

"While you were outside talking to AJ, I had a friendly visit with Crystal and Matt—that's what the senator insisted I call him," Maggie said, adding an eye roll. "I let him think that I'm his newest fan. Anyway, the day before Benny died, he told the senator he'd mailed a copy of his report up to that point. Now, the senator is worried that there might be *another* copy floating around. He doesn't want the information leaked to the press before he makes his recommendation. He hinted that once he has the information, he's hoping he can plan a big event, maybe a ribbon cutting ceremony with balloons and food and the high school band. He promised to send me an invitation."

"Were you flirting with him, Mags?"

She waved her hand, dismissing my question. "Of course not. It was all innocent. I pretended to be an avid admirer of his wonderful political works. If my eyelashes fluttered, it was a total accident."

I had to laugh at that comment. "You don't know the first thing about Senator Nash, do you?"

She raised her eyebrows. "I know he supports the construction of a golf course on land that should stay undeveloped. That's all I need to know at this point. But I did a good job convincing him that I think he's brilliant."

"And his assistant, Crystal? Did she fall for it, too?"

"I had to be really sneaky. She's like an eagle keeping watch over him."

"Well done, I guess. Isn't it convenient about the report? If he has the only copy, and Benny is dead, the senator could make up anything."

"Exactly," Maggie said, banging her hands on the steering wheel for emphasis. "And, he suggested in a very roundabout way that Benny's friend might have been given a copy of the report that hasn't surfaced yet."

"Benny's friend, Sunny?"

"I assume so. At any rate, it didn't seem like a good idea for Sunny to innocently walk into the inn and get hijacked by that duo. Nash has a lot of power and what does Sunny have? Just us at this point. It didn't take much convincing for her to agree with the plan, but I had to figure out how to make it look like she'd disappeared. That's where Jasper comes in." Maggie turned into the driveway at Sea Breeze and parked behind Luke's truck.

I thought about what Maggie just told me. "How will we hide Sunny and a gigantic dog?"

Maggie's grin told me there was more to her plan. "That's what you'll find out when we get inside, Dani."

I really didn't need any more surprises.

I had plenty on my plate.

30

*P*ip, Jasper, and I followed Maggie into Sea Breeze, normally my sanctuary at the end of a stressful day, but tonight? I suspected it would be anything but with Sunny's arrival throwing a monkey wrench into my world.

As soon as Jasper entered, her nose tipped up in the air, she sniffed, and made a beeline straight to the kitchen.

Happy voices welcomed her arrival.

"Jasper!"

Sunny sank to the floor and buried her face in Jasper's thick fur. Her tail, waving back and forth, created such a breeze that all the papers on my counter fluttered to the floor.

Rose nodded for me to follow her into the living

room with Luke and Maggie.

"Did you tell her the plan?" Rose asked Maggie.

Maggie collapsed in a heap on the sofa with her feet stretched out like she'd made a soft landing. "Only the part about Sunny disappearing, but not where she'll actually be hiding out."

"Yoo-hoo!" Sue Ellen's voice rang out in her crystal-clear sing-song tone from the front entryway. "Where is everyone?" She swept into my living room, wearing a red tunic over white leggings, with bright red toenails peeking from her open-toed sandals. If nothing else, Sue Ellen Baer's arrival always added an exclamation point to a situation.

This time, her arrival made me suspicious.

"Where are my guests?" Sue Ellen dropped her giant leather tote on a chair and looked around the room. "I have a room all ready and waiting, and the backyard is being reinforced with extra privacy fencing as we speak. I had to call in some favors to get that done quickly, but don't worry, everything is almost set for a super disappearing act. Aren't they here yet?"

"Take a deep breath, Sue Ellen," I said, as I put two and two together and finally understood the plan. "Are you referring to Sunny and Jasper? They're in the kitchen."

"Oh, bless your heart, Dani," she wiped her brow theatrically. "I was afraid you were going to tell me that the plan got sabotaged just when I was so looking forward to their company." She dug around in her bag and held up a baggie. "I brought treats for Jasper. I want to make sure she takes a liking to me," she said as she sashayed into the kitchen.

"*That's* your plan, Mags?" I asked after I heard Sue Ellen chatting with her soon-to-be guests about fences and food preferences and six-hundred-thread-count sheets. I rolled my eyes. "She'll want to have a party with Sunny as the guest of honor. How will *that* help?"

"Oh, come on, Dani," Rose said. "Sue Ellen can keep a secret if she has to. She's thrilled to be helping out. What was *your* plan? To have Sunny and Jasper stay here where people come and go like Grand Central Station?"

I had to admit my grandma had a very valid point. AJ would be the first to stop by, especially after Lily told him that Sunny hadn't been abducted. Let everyone else assume she'd been kidnapped, but it wouldn't have been fair to deceive AJ. He could know she was safe, but it was better to have her tucked out of the way somewhere besides my home.

If he showed up, it might send Sunny into a real disappearing act.

I crossed my arms and said, "What about Luke's Blueberry Acres Farm? At least there, Jasper could have some real freedom outside." Even I heard the poutiness in my voice. Not something to be proud of.

"Probably the second place people would think to look," Rose said. "Who will suspect they'll be hiding out at Sue Ellen's house? It's perfect."

"Time will tell," I said without much enthusiasm. Something felt off about the whole scheme, but I couldn't put my finger on it. It could just be the fact that when Sue Ellen was involved, there was a strong possibility that something would go wrong.

"How about," Maggie said to me, "you and I bring Sunny and Jasper over to Sue Ellen's house and make sure it really is suitable for them." She raised her eyebrows expectantly, waiting for an answer.

I looked at Luke. He nodded, apparently agreeing with Maggie's suggestion. "Just for the record, it's the last thing I want to do, but, okay. I feel like I'm outnumbered on this. We'll take them over, check out the situation, and I'll come back home," I checked my watch, "in time for a glass of wine and dinner."

"Don't worry. I'll have a glass of merlot and my famous sausage pizza ready and waiting for you," Luke said, dazzling me with his heartwarming smile. "Just send me a text when you're leaving Sue Ellen's house so the pizza will be hot out of the oven when you get home." He massaged my shoulders making me wish for nothing more than settling in a chair with my feet up. "I know you've had a long day, Dani, but in the end, you'll be glad you did this so you can relax instead of fretting and pacing all night."

He knew me too well. And the idea of his cheesy, garlicky, hot Italian sausage pizza already had me drooling for a slice. If I tried extra hard, I could almost taste the delicious gooey pie.

"Sue Ellen? Sunny? Are you ready to go?" I called into the kitchen. The sooner we left, the sooner I'd be back to actually taste my dinner instead of just teasing myself with the thought of it.

Pip, sensing something was happening, dashed from the kitchen with Jasper hot on her heels. I laughed at the sight of my ten-pound terrier leading her giant new friend. What a combination!

Sue Ellen, with her arm around Sunny, followed the four-legged pair. "All set. Are you coming with us, too?"

"Yup," Maggie said. "Dani and I want to make sure that backyard is secure for Jasper."

"Oh," Sue Ellen waved the comment away. "Nine Pine Nursery is the best when it comes to fencing. And, I only hire the best."

A shock went up my spine.

"Nine Pine Nursery?" Sunny froze and turned white as a sheet. "Hunter Bodane? Isn't the whole point of me going missing to keep me hidden from the people involved with the project so they can't come after me?"

"Oh dear." Sue Ellen fidgeted. "Did I do something wrong?"

"Of course not," Rose assured her while she patted her back. "You didn't know. I'm sure it will be fine. He's all done, right?"

"Well, I think so." Now, Sue Ellen wasn't so sure of her perfect situation.

"What if he's still there?" Sunny asked. "I may as well just go back to my own house." She crossed her arms defiantly. "At least I'd have Tilly across the street for backup. What do I have at Sue Ellen's house besides Jasper?"

"My whole house has an alarm system. You'll be safe." Sue Ellen sounded like she was about to cry at this turn of events.

"I can stay if that makes you feel any better," Maggie said. "Just consider me a younger version of Tilly."

"That's settled, then," I said before anyone had time to offer up more potential problems. I wanted this show on the road and someone had to take charge. "Maggie stays with Sue Ellen and Sunny. I'll swing by first thing in the morning."

Maggie opened the door, ushering a reluctant Sunny and Jasper to her car.

Sue Ellen held me back. "Dani?" she said. "I might have told that Hunter guy that he had to make the fence secure enough to hold a big Newfoundland. Do you think he'll put it all together?"

Of course he would. "We'll reassess in the morning, okay? With your alarm and Maggie keeping watch, tonight should be fine. Just don't let Sunny go outside by herself." I sounded confident but didn't feel very assured.

Sue Ellen nodded. I could tell her initial excitement had been for entertaining a houseguest and now her plans resembled a lock down.

I knew there'd be a problem, I just hadn't expected it to lead a potential murderer right to Sunny.

31

When I opened my eyes in the morning, sunshine streamed through my window. At least the blue sky promised a gorgeous day even if everything around me was headed into the eye of a storm.

Pip snagged my blanket with her teeth and pulled it down.

"Hey, what do you think you're doing?" I tried to get my blanket back, but Pip took this as the beginning of a great game of tug of war.

I pulled.

She fake-growled.

I laughed.

She shook her head ferociously, and I gave in to her antics knowing it was a battle I never won.

"What's all the noise up here?" Luke poked his head around our bedroom door. "Oh, it's just you two. I thought there was an intruder I had to chase away."

I knew he wasn't really worried about an intruder here, but it was a gentle reminder for me to get up and head to Sue Ellen's house. When I'd left Maggie in charge of keeping Sunny and Jasper safe last night, I'd promised to return in the morning.

"Want me to come with you?" he asked.

"I'd love that. Once we have everything squared away," I wiggled my eyebrows, "maybe we can sneak off for our picnic that got waylaid on Thursday.

"In that case, I'll stay here and pack a romantic picnic," Luke said, sending me his most expressive wink. My heart fluttered helplessly. Sometimes I still had to pinch myself at my good fortune of sharing my life with this wonderful, kind person.

Luke clapped his hands, putting an end to my daydreaming. "Get out of bed sleepyhead. I have a pot of mint tea ready for you and warm apple muffins. That should keep you going until you get to Sue Ellen's house. I'm sure she'll have a breakfast feast for her guests so leave room and give yourself enough time to enjoy her food."

While Luke gave his good-natured lecture, I half

listened as I pulled on comfy jeans and a Little Dog Diner t-shirt. "It's a good thing I have the weekend off, but it's not how we planned to spend our free time, is it?" I felt terrible that we'd only managed to do the helicopter ride so far and we'd had to push the rest of Luke's well-thought-out plans to the back burner.

In the kitchen, I poured tea into my travel cup and wrapped a warm muffin in a napkin.

Pip looked at me from her spot at the French doors overlooking Blueberry Bay. "Sorry, Pipsqueak. I don't have time for our morning jog on the beach, but I'll make it up to you. You can play with Jasper. How does that sound?"

Pip yipped her approval and ran to the front door.

"How does she understand you?" Luke said with a half-grin and a shake of his head.

"It's simple—I talk, and she listens."

Luke broke into a roar of laughter. "I hope you aren't trying to tell *me* something."

I gave him my best silly look—crossed eyes and fish lips—which made him laugh even harder. I hugged him and whispered, "I can't imagine what you're talking about. You're perfect just the way you are."

With Pip in the passenger seat of my dark green MG, I juggled my tea while stuffing the delicious muffin in my mouth. Pip licked her lips. "Not gonna happen, Pipster. You'll have to wait for Sue Ellen's gourmet doggy treats."

I pulled into Sue Ellen's circular drive and parked behind Maggie's Jeep. At least she hadn't lost her patience with Sue Ellen's special brand of over-bearing southern charm and stormed out before now. Maybe she'd brought earplugs; or, the food was too good. Knowing Maggie, that had to be it.

Pip dashed to the kitchen and scratched at the door of one of her favorite spots.

Sue Ellen opened the door dressed in red jeans and a tunic I hadn't seen before, a riot of red and white flowers cascading down the front. "Pippy!" she said, her arms open in welcome. "You couldn't wait to visit with your new friend?" She stepped aside as we followed the delicious smells.

Luke had been right about a breakfast feast. Trays of fruit, muffins, scones, and a selection of hot and cold beverages filled her island. "Are you expecting more company?" I asked, wondering how the four of us would make even the tiniest dent in this spread.

Sunny, with her back to me, stood at Sue Ellen's

stove, flipping pancakes. "Who wants them hot off the griddle?" she shouted.

Without hesitation, Maggie thrust her plate in Sunny's direction. "I'm not shy. Pile 'em on."

Sunny laughed and heaped six pancakes on Maggie's plate. "How about you, Dani? I have two more hot blueberry pancakes looking for a hungry stomach."

"Perfect," I said as I watched Maggie pour about a pint of maple syrup on her stack before she sat at the kitchen table. Pip made a beeline to Maggie's side sitting next to Jasper as the two, no doubt, hoped for a handout or a spill.

"I settled across from Maggie and drained the last bit of syrup from the container. "Did you all have a quiet night?"

"A-huh," she mumbled around her mouthful of food.

"Sue Ellen? Do you have any more of those gourmet dog treats? I promised Pip you'd spoil her when we got here."

"Of course." She carried a red plate overflowing with cookies to the table. They looked good enough for us to eat. She held two out and lured Jasper and Pip to the door that led to the backyard. "Come on, you two. Out you go. No more begging for pancakes."

Sunny set Sue Ellen's plate next to Maggie, then sat next to me, her own plate towering with pancakes.

"You'd better hurry up and get back here, Sue Ellen," she called. "Maggie's eyeing your breakfast. You might have to fight her off."

Maggie aimed her fork toward Sue Ellen's top pancake, but Sue Ellen, with a quickness that surprised me, pulled her plate out of reach. "I don't think so, Maggie. You can make your own if you want any more."

Maggie groaned and whined. "You know I can't cook to save my life. Just one more? Please?"

Sue Ellen laughed and sacrificed her top pancake to the woman with a bottomless stomach. "There. If that doesn't fill you up, nothing will. Now let me eat in peace."

With my plate clean, I poured myself a cup of tea and wandered to the window. I laughed at the dogs. Jasper, with her front paws down and her tail high in the air, barely moved as Pip ran circles around her.

Suddenly, Jasper charged toward the gate with an earth-trembling woof.

"What's going on?" I asked, straining my neck to

see around the corner of the house. "Did you hear Jasper?"

Sunny leaped to the window and craned her neck to see as much of the backyard as possible.

"Oh no! Hunter Bodane just walked into the fenced area. What's he doing here?" Sunny shrank away from the window and slid to the floor.

"Oh dear," Sue Ellen said, marching to the door. "I'll find out what's going on."

I walked outside too, not trusting her ability to keep our secret.

"Mornin', Hunter," she said with an extra dose of southern accent. "Are you checking your work-manship?"

"Oh, hi, Sue Ellen. Actually, I think I may have dropped my favorite hammer when I was working here yesterday. Thought I could take a look without disturbing you."

Jasper and Pip sniffed around his work boots. "Is this Sunny's dog?"

Without skipping a beat, Sue Ellen said, "Didn't you hear? Jasper was wandering on Main Street yesterday and no one knows *what* happened to poor Sunny. That girl has been through so much I offered to keep her dog safe until..."

I forced a serious expression instead of smiling at

Sue Ellen's quick and clever answer. Leaving her thought unfinished added an appropriate sense of drama. Perfect.

"Oh, I didn't know."

Yeah, right. "There's your hammer." I pointed to the patio table. Looked to me like he'd left it on purpose to give himself an excuse to return and poke around.

Hunter smacked the side of his head like he was the most forgetful person around. I didn't fall for it. "Thanks," he said. "I'm heading over to the Blue Moon Inn to lead a group around my property before our brunch. Senator Nash has to make his recommendation, and I'm hoping it will be positive." He tucked his hammer in the loop on his pant leg. "Well, I hope Sunny turns up."

"Sure he does," I said to Sue Ellen after Hunter left. "Did you notice how he kept looking in your windows? Good thing Sunny stayed out of sight and your explanation about Jasper was perfect."

Sue Ellen beamed from my compliment. "Why, bless your heart, Dani. Sometimes I can actually manage to say the right thing without hemming and hawing and tripping over my own tongue."

"Yes, you can. Now, let's put our heads together

and figure out how to find out what Senator Nash is going to propose for the Nine Pine Nursery land."

"Something undercover?" Sue Ellen asked with way too much enthusiasm.

"Nothing like that. Sunny knows the area. Let's find out what suggestions she has.

32

*I*nside, Sunny paced across Sue Ellen's spacious kitchen like a trapped tiger.

Maggie held her gun but quickly returned it to her holster when I told her that Hunter had gone. She snickered at Sue Ellen's innocent sounding, yet clever explanation of Jasper's presence in the backyard.

"Sue Ellen was amazing," I said and, as I expected, our hostess puffed up like a proud mama dove.

"It's only a matter of time," Sunny sounded totally defeated, "before one of them figures out I'm not really missing. They'll come back looking for me now that they know Jasper is here. I'd rather be out and about instead of slinking behind a locked door."

"It's your call, Sunny," I said. "We need your help. Hunter is leading Senator Nash and the others involved in the golf course project on a tour of his land. Apparently, even with two of the participants dead, Hunter at least, is hoping someone else will step up and buy his property. Is there any way we can, you know, accidentally on purpose bump into them?"

Sunny's face broke into a wide grin. "Absolutely. There's a trail that meanders along the bayside of the property that I used when I was a kid. It connects with conservation land and is kind of overgrown now. It would be easy to say we lost our way and accidentally headed in the wrong direction. But there's no guarantee you'll bump into them."

"It's worth a try. At least it gives us a better idea of what the property is all about," I said. "Who's coming?"

Three me's rang out in unison.

"Are you sure, Sunny?"

She nodded.

Was that a good idea for her to come along? Maybe, maybe not. It was hard to predict when we were flying by the seat of our pants.

"I'll pack some food. That way it will look like we planned a hike and a picnic," Sue Ellen said.

A picnic without Luke? *That* wasn't part of my plan.

"Hey," Maggie elbowed me in my side, "don't wimp out on me now. Focus, Dani." She gave me a look like I'd sprouted a couple of horns or something.

"What? Do I have syrup on my face?" I wiped the edges of my mouth. "Or, blueberries stuck between my teeth?" I bared my teeth for her to inspect.

"Ewww! No! Please close your mouth. You drifted off somewhere, and I need you here," she jabbed at herself, "with me if we expect to have any luck crashing Hunter's tour to hear what they're up to." She put her hands on both sides of my face and stared at me. "Good. You're back. Now stay here and quit dreaming about Luke."

"I wasn't!" I lied.

Maggie gave me her award-winning eye roll. "Don't lie when I heard you say, a picnic without Luke wasn't part of your plan."

"I said that out loud?" I wished I could break that lousy habit of mine.

"Uh-huh."

Sue Ellen set a red backpack on the island with a thud. "Who wants to be the pack horse?"

"I don't mind," Sunny offered. "It will make me

look legitimate."

"Look legitimately lost?" Maggie asked. "How will you explain that if you know the land so well?"

Sunny shrugged. "I'll figure out something. Let's get going or we'll miss the whole show."

We all piled into Maggie's Jeep with the two dogs in the way back much to their displeasure. It couldn't be helped. Pip could fit between Sunny and me but there wasn't enough room for Jasper on the seat. "Keep your friend company back there," I said to Pip when she put her front paws on the back of my seat like she was ready to hop over.

She yipped and kept her feet where they were.

Sunny gave Maggie directions into a small pull-off hidden in a dense thicket of twisted evergreens.

Jasper's woof of excitement shook the Jeep.

"She knows where we are," Sunny said, jumping out of the car and opening the back to let the dogs out. "I've brought her here a few times." She heaved the backpack on and waited for the rest of us.

"Wait!" Sue Ellen said to Sunny. "I stuffed a pair of comfy walking shoes in the backpack. I need to change."

"Really Sue Ellen?" Maggie asked without hiding her annoyance. "You didn't take care of that *before* we left?"

"I didn't know if you would stop somewhere on the way," she said defensively. "What if I ran into someone I knew? I like everything to match." Maggie aimed her fob at the door and unlocked the Jeep so Sue Ellen could sit down, change her footwear, and stash her sandals inside.

"Ready now?" Maggie asked after Sue Ellen finished tying her red canvas sneakers that looked like they'd never been worn.

With a wide smile, Sue Ellen beamed at us. "Ready for anything."

I doubted that but wasn't going to spoil her mood.

"Jasper took off," Sunny said. "I'm sure she's following the trail we usually take, which will bring us onto the Nine Pine Nursery land. Let's go."

Pushing branches out of the way and stepping over rocks and dead limbs on what once must have been a good walking trail, we slowly followed Sunny.

"Are you sure you know where you're going?" Sue Ellen said after stopping to catch her breath.

"You can wait here if you want to," Sunny answered without stopping.

That got Sue Ellen moving. This adventure was turning into more work than she'd expected but getting left behind was definitely not on her agenda.

Finally, after slow progress, the trail opened up to a clearing with a stunning view of Blueberry Bay.

"Amazing," I said but refused to join the others at the edge of a cliff. The sound of surf crashing below activated a touch of vertigo. "I'll stay back here."

Pip, who must have followed Jasper, startled me when she leaped against my legs. I sat down, letting her jump in my lap and shower my face with a good cleaning. "Where's Jasper?" I asked her.

Pip ran off but stopped and looked back at us. "Pip's trying to tell us to follow her," I said to the others.

"Now, we're on Nine Pine Nursery land," Sunny said. "This is what the conservation group wants to add to their parcel.

We followed Pip. In the distance, four figures stood in a group angled away from us. As we came closer to the group, the wind carried Crystal's voice straight to us.

She held up an envelope. "And this arrived from Benny. Senator Nash said to wait until we were all here, in this spectacular setting, before I opened it to share with you. But first, a moment of silence to remember our dear friends Benny Chadman and Josh Whiting."

They all bowed their heads and, as silently as possible, we inched closer.

"I don't see Jasper," Sunny whispered to me.

"We'll find her, don't worry," I answered, hoping what I said was true.

Crystal raised her head and solemnly opened the envelope, slipping the contents out. She cleared her throat. "I don't believe it." She looked at the others. "Benny's report says the land is *not* suitable for a golf course."

Hunter snatched the papers from her.

"What do you think you're doing?" Crystal screeched, then she lunged to get the papers back.

Hunter held them out of her reach, looked at them, and then tossed them into the breeze.

"You can't do that!" With her arms flying in every direction, Crystal tried to catch the papers as the wind blew them here and there.

I looked at Sunny who stood staring at the scene with an expression of shock and disbelief etched on her face. I nudged her. "That's good news, right?"

"Oh, yeah," she answered more like a robot than someone who should be thrilled with this outcome.

"No golf course. Maybe the conservation group has a shot now," I said, hoping to spur her out of her fog.

"Maybe."

I forced her to look at me. "What the heck is wrong?"

"I'm not sure. It's... um... not what I expected to hear."

"Hey!" Hunter shouted. "What are you doing here?"

I wasn't sure why we hadn't been spotted sooner, but now we had some explaining to do. I stepped forward. "We're looking for Jasper. Have you seen her?"

Hunter sneered. "First it's Sunny who went missing and now it's her big dog? Who are you trying to kid? Get off my land."

"Hunter, wait!" Crystal yelled to his back as he stomped off. "We'll figure something out. It's not the end of the world."

"It's the end of my patience. I want all of you off my land." he pointed at each of us. "Now."

I took Sunny's arm and got her moving back toward Maggie's Jeep. Pip took the lead so even if Sunny couldn't think straight, I was confident that my terrier would get us away from this unexpected situation.

How did this influence the murders?

33

We found Jasper waiting next to Maggie's Jeep. The return walk, as usually happens when you know where you're going, seemed quicker.

Sunny rushed to her dog's side, hugging her, and burying her face in the thick fur. "Oh, Jasper. I was so worried."

Maybe that explained Sunny's strange reaction to Crystal's announcement about the negative conclusion of Benny's report. She was distracted with worry.

Maybe.

Before Sunny got in the Jeep, I asked her if there was something else on her mind.

"Something's not right about that report Crystal read," she answered, sliding onto the back seat.

"What are you talking about?"

"I'll tell you when we get back to the inn." She turned her face toward the window, giving me the brush-off.

Well that told me absolutely nothing, but it sure got my curiosity ramped into overdrive. What could possibly be wrong with the report? Was it fake? But who would know with Benny dead? Unless... Sunny knew more than she'd admitted to us.

Her face, still turned toward the window, gave me no clue about what she might be thinking. I'd have to be patient.

I chuckled at *that* thought.

"What's so funny back there?" Maggie asked, looking at me in the rearview mirror. "You two have been silent, and now Dani is laughing. Share it with us."

Sue Ellen turned around. "Why so glum, Sunny? I thought you'd be kicking up your heels and doing a jig with that negative report. Isn't that what you wanted all along?"

Sunny sucked in a lungful of air and let it out in one big huff. "Yes and no. Okay. Here's the thing.

Benny *didn't* find any reason to halt the golf course project."

"What? He told you that?" I asked. Her admission stunned me into silence.

"The reason he was making that last boat trip was because he wanted more photos from the water in case he'd missed something. He wanted to stop the project with all his heart, but he wouldn't submit a false report. Benny was known for his honesty."

"And he never got a chance to take more photos," I said. "But what did he tell you about his findings?"

"It's not what he told me. It's what he gave me."

"You have his report?"

"His preliminary report. The one he told me to keep in case—"

"Something happened to him?" I asked.

Sunny nodded.

"Why was he worried?"

She shrugged. "He knew someone would be disappointed in whatever result he found. With so much money involved—millions—he was realistic and held a healthy amount of caution. He figured if I had a copy of his report, it would at least protect the integrity of his work and maybe prevent someone from harming him."

"Did someone find it when your house got trashed?"

She shook her head.

"Sunny? You sent me on a wild goose chase for that report? You said it was on your kitchen counter when all along, you knew it wasn't there?"

She nodded. "I'll explain when we get to the inn. "I promise. I'll tell you everything I know."

I slid away from her as far as possible, fuming about the deception. "Let me ask you this? Why did you come to the Little Dog Diner looking for me after you swam to shore?"

"I'd read about you and the Little Dog Diner in the Blueberry Bay Grapevine and how you've helped solve mysteries. I didn't know where else to turn once I found myself in your town."

"Benny didn't send you?"

"No." Her voice was somber. "I had to make a decision. I like the name of your diner and decided it was my best choice. I figured you must love dogs as much as I do so we had something in common from the start."

That I could relate to, but the rest? "Why should we believe you now after all the lies you've told us?" I was furious. "We've protected you, hidden you, fed you, run your errands. We've even found a place for you to stay because we *believed* you. But it was all based on lies. How will we ever know what's true? How do we know *you* didn't kill Benny before you jumped overboard?"

There it was, what I'd suspected all along, out in the open.

Sunny's head dropped into her hands and she mumbled, "I didn't kill him. He was my best friend. We *did* argue about his report, and that's why I went into the cabin. I was mad at him for being so honest when he could have blurred the lines a little. In hindsight, that argument probably saved my life."

She sobbed what sounded like genuine tears, but honestly? I wasn't sure.

We were a quiet group that trooped into Sue Ellen's house after I let the two dogs in the backyard.

"Okay, Sunny. Here's your chance to tell us what you know and convince us that we should believe this new version." I knew I sounded mean, but she had to understand this was her last chance. If she got it wrong *this* time, she'd have no one fighting on her side.

"I have to go upstairs for something," she said, her voice full of apology. It seemed as though Sunny was asking permission to leave our sight.

"Okay." I waved my hand toward the door. "Go." If she didn't come back that was okay with me, too.

Sunny pushed through the kitchen door, letting it swing closed behind her.

"You don't mean that, Dani," Maggie said.

"Mean what?"

"That you don't care if she comes back."

Another slip of my tongue? Well, now everyone knew exactly how I felt. But did I really not care? Of course, I couldn't turn my back on her. I liked Sunny Shaw and her dog Jasper. That's what made all this so much more painful. I wanted her to convince us that she could tell the truth. Every bit of it.

Sue Ellen flitted around her kitchen, putting the kettle on, arranging food on plates, but I tuned out her small talk with Maggie. All I cared about was Sunny's story.

She quickly returned with an envelope and tossed it on the island. "Here's what Benny left with me. Read it and then we can talk."

With trembling fingers, I slid the papers out and unfolded them. At the top, in big, bold, black letters was the word APPROVED. I looked up at the others. "Benny approved the golf course project?"

Sunny nodded. "He found nothing to stop it. No

endangered plants or birds or runoff issues. Nothing. It wasn't what he wanted, but it was what he found."

"I don't understand. What was the report that Crystal read? That one said the project was denied." Maggie ripped the papers from my hand. "Something's wrong somewhere."

I looked at Sunny. "Why did you hide this report and lie to the police that you didn't have anything from Benny?"

"Isn't it obvious?"

I stared at her wondering where this was going.

"Benny wouldn't send a false report but if there was *no* report, I thought the project would have to start back at square one with a new study giving the conservation group more time to convince Hunter to sell to them."

"But why send me to get the report if you had it hidden somewhere?"

"I thought it made sense for everyone to think there was a report floating around. It would keep them busy looking and wondering what Benny found. Keep everyone a little off balance."

"And you in danger," I said. "So, Crystal read a fake report. And now *we* have the real one." I held it up. "But, how can we prove it?"

Sunny tossed something else on the table—a

waterproof bag. "A flash drive from Benny's computer. I saved it before I tossed his computer overboard. That should be enough proof for you to believe me now."

She didn't even attempt to hide her defiant tone. I liked it and it gave me something I could believe in.

"Okay, here's the thing," I said. "I promised to help Lily with her brunch. If we all go, we can do some brainstorming about everyone involved in the golf course project. We know the report is fake so if we're extra vigilant, and luck is on our side, one of them will reveal their hand." I looked around the kitchen. "Are you all with me?"

Of course, they all nodded.

"Let's go." I led the way, bringing Pip but leaving Jasper in Sue Ellen's house. I didn't want to, but we had no choice.

34

*I*nstead of going through the front door of the Blue Moon Inn, I led the way around to the side, hoping to avoid interrupting Senator Nash's brunch.

"I wasn't sure I'd have extra help," Lily said as she stirred a pot on the stove.

The chowder aroma jogged my memory, filling me with guilt.

"Rose brought it over," Lily said as she followed my gaze. "I called last night to remind you, and she said she'd take care of it."

"Is she here?"

"Yes. She's setting the table while my guests chat in the sitting room. They were all cheerful this morning, but now, after their tour of Hunter's property, it's more like a funeral in there. What happened?" Lily moved the pot off the stove.

"You fill her in, Dani," Maggie said. "I'll be in Lily's office doing some brainstorming with Sunny and Sue Ellen."

I shared the details with Lily, then joined Maggie, Sunny, and Sue Ellen.

Maggie held Sunny in a piercing gaze. "I have to know," Maggie said, "where did you hide Benny's report and the flash drive? Your house was trashed. Dani and I saw the mess. Anyone who knew what they were looking for would have found that report."

Sunny smiled like she had a delicious secret. The first upbeat emotion I'd seen all day. "Before I left with Benny, I zipped it inside Jasper's dog bed."

After a moment of dumbfounded silence, we all burst out laughing.

"Dani and Luke arrived just in time to get my clothes and Jasper's dog bed and beat the person who vandalized my house. The next day?" She lifted her shoulders and puckered her mouth. "Would have been too late."

"And the flash drive?" I asked.

"I had that waterproof bag with me on the boat with my license and some money. I always take it when I'm on the water. It comes in handy," she said.

"Okay," Maggie said, getting her laughter under control. "That was some really smart thinking on your part. Now, let's get to work and figure out motives."

Sue Ellen pulled her red leather-bound note-book and a pen from her tote bag. "Ready," she said with her pen poised for action.

"Sunny?" Maggie said. "You know everyone better than we do. Who, on the golf course project, wanted Benny dead?"

Sue Ellen waved her arm in the air. "Wait. I have a question. What about someone else? Shouldn't we consider that? Did Benny have any enemies?"

"Not that I'm aware of," Sunny said. "Everyone liked Benny. To *your* question, Maggie, my first suspect was Josh, but he's dead, not that it rules him out as Benny's killer though, right?"

"That's a good point," I said, warming up to Sunny's train of thought. "There could be two killers involved in this mystery."

"I think," Sunny continued after a bit of hesitation, "that Hunter Bodane had the most to lose in dollars and cents if the project didn't move forward. When he bought the Nine Pine Nursery, he gambled on his grand vision. He took out a gigantic loan and upgraded everything, from the retail building to a top of the line new greenhouse, plus acres of the newest and most expensive plant inventory. He wanted to attract the high-end customers and sell at tip top prices."

"I take it he lost on that risky plan," I said, doing a mental calculation in my head. I was well aware of investing in a business, risk taking, and the cost of overhead. One wrong choice and everything could fall apart quickly.

"Big time. He's desperate to sell before he has to declare bankruptcy and the golf course was going to be his ticket out of debt, leaving him with a healthy chunk to start something else."

"But Benny gave the project a green light and they were friends, so why would Hunter kill him?" I couldn't get my head wrapped around how this all turned into a double homicide.

"That's true," Sunny said, "but I don't know if anyone but me knew that. *I* think everyone expected Benny to find something to interfere with the plan. I mean, you all saw that property. It's gorgeous. It should stay in its natural state. Even with Benny's stellar reputation, I suspect someone didn't trust he'd submit an honest report if he didn't actually find a legitimate reason to stop the golf course."

"I can see that scenario," I said, "but if Hunter's

whole strategy hinged on having the golf course move forward, he wouldn't kill Josh."

"Whoever killed Josh either hated him or wanted the golf course development stopped," Sunny said. "I tend to think that someone like Josh Whiting had a lot of enemies so maybe these two murders aren't even connected."

Sue Ellen scribbled furiously. "I have a question," she said. "Benny's killer had to have access to a boat. Did Hunter have a boat?"

"Great question." I was impressed that she was the only one to think of that important detail. "Sunny? Do you know?"

"I don't know if he owned a boat but lots of people around Blueberry Bay have a connection to someone who does. The thing is, though, Hunter is *always* at the nursery working. Especially in the morning. He's obsessed about having everything perfect when he opens for business."

Sue Ellen drew a double line under what she'd written. "Okay. Hunter's probably a no," she said. "Who's next?"

"How about Officer Mick Walker," Maggie suggested. "He always seemed to show up when something was happening. He came to the diner looking for Sunny after the murder. He was at her house when Dani and Luke went to pick up a change of clothes and also when Sunny reported the break-in. He's part of the golf course project. Why would he want Benny dead?" She looked at Sunny.

"In my opinion, Mick is a wild card. He always looks out for himself. Like I said before, he's probably hoping for a better paying position in the golf course hierarchy in exchange for helping push any permits or other pesky barriers through the system. Being a town cop isn't glamourous enough for him. And yes, Sue Ellen, before you ask, the police do have a boat he could have used."

I thought about Sunny's explanation. "The next question then is, would he benefit even if the golf course failed?"

"A guy like Mick would figure out how to make it work for him," Sunny said.

"Maybe," I said, "if Mick killed Benny and Josh found out, Mick had to take care of him too, to save his own skin and sacrifice the golf course project."

"I can see him bending the rules," Maggie said, "but a killer? I find that hard to swallow."

Sue Ellen drew another dark line across the page. "Mick Walker, fifty-fifty. Next?"

"Crystal Wilson, assistant to Senator Nash," Maggie said. "She strikes me as someone capable of anything. Her fingerprints are on every piece of the project and, I'm going out on a limb here—I think she'd do *anything* to get what she wants."

Sunny nodded. "I think you're right about that and she'd definitely have friends with powerful boats, plus, she makes her own schedule."

Sue Ellen looked up. "Did you see her face when she read that report? I thought she was going to jump over the edge of the cliff and put herself out of her misery. I'd guess she wanted Benny out of the way to hide a negative report."

"I don't think Crystal cared one way or the other about the golf course. I mean, whatever happened, she'd wiggle her way to the front of the line for publicity. It's not about the money for her, it's the recognition. Maybe she saw more benefit for herself if the land stayed undeveloped," Sunny said. "That would explain why she didn't just throw the report away. I don't believe for one minute that she didn't look at it before she opened it in front of the others."

"You mean it was an act?" Sue Ellen asked, stunned from that revelation.

"A good one, too," I said.

"She can still throw the report away," Maggie said. "I suspect she thinks she got what she wanted from it and that's the last anyone will hear about Benny's report. She doesn't have to make it public."

"But we heard her read it," Sunny said. "Are you saying that now the killer will be shutting all of us up?"

"Who would believe us?" I asked. "What we know, and the killer knows, is that the report Crystal read is a phony. For some reason, someone fabricated that report and sent it to the senator's office. That's what we have to use to our advantage."

Sue Ellen clicked her pen several times. "I'm putting Crystal as a strong possibility. Now, what about the senator? We didn't talk about him yet."

"Senator Nash," Sunny said thoughtfully. "From what Benny told me, he believed the golf course was a good idea, but he was concerned about the environmental impact. That's why he hired Benny to do the study. He's a politician, an idea guy. I'm sure he has a folder full of other possibilities for that land if the golf course falls through."

"Senator Nash," Sue Ellen said. "I don't know what to write next to his name except that anything is possible."

"Two murders and four possible suspects. Who did it?" I asked.

I didn't expect an answer.

35

*L*ily peeked around her office door. "Dani? I could use some help serving."

I jumped up, startling poor Pip. She looked around for the cause of this sudden emergency.

"Sorry, Pipsqueak. You'd better stay in here out of the way."

She jumped onto Sue Ellen's lap and refused to look at me. Ah, the guilt trip from a ten-pound terrier was worse than from my two-legged friends. I told myself that she'd get over it.

I followed Lily into the kitchen. "What's the plan?"

"Rose just served drinks to everyone along with baskets of rolls. You can bring the salads out, then we'll serve the chowder. I want to keep the food moving at a leisurely pace, so they have time to talk."

"Have you heard anything interesting?"

"Hunter is pushing for a different developer who he says is interested in a smaller golf course to adjust for the environmental impact. I think that means he'll leave a bigger buffer between the course and Blueberry Bay. But Senator Nash sounds like he's getting cold feet."

After covering my t-shirt with a white button-down shirt, I picked up a big tray that held all the salads and pushed through the door into the dining room.

"It's just too soon after our losses," I heard Senator Nash say. "We need to be respectful."

I set the first salad in front of Hunter just as he slammed his hand on the table.

Startled, my hands jerked, almost sending the tray and remaining salads to the floor.

"With all due respect, Senator, I don't have time to be respectful. If this drags out any longer, I'll be bankrupt. Is that what you want on your conscience? With a sale soon, everyone makes out," Hunter said as he glared across the table.

I moved slowly, serving the salads, and hoping

no one would pay attention to me so I could hear more of their conversation.

"It makes me wonder," Mick said, "how you found this new developer so quickly, Hunter. With Benny and Josh dead, you magically have someone else lined up? Maybe this was your plan all along." He stabbed his fork into a plump cherry tomato and popped it in his mouth.

Hunter's mouth, on the other hand, dropped open. "What are you trying to say, Officer? Just spit it out. Let's clear the air."

Mick smirked before speaking. "I'm also wondering where you were Thursday morning when Benny was murdered. Without an alibi, I think I'll suggest to Detective Crenshaw here in Misty Harbor that he put you under a microscope."

Hunter threw his napkin on the table. "I'm not listening to anymore of this. I don't need any of you to approve of who I decide to sell my property to." He stood, pushing his chair back so quickly, it toppled over with a loud clunk.

Senator Nash held his hand up. "Wait a minute, Hunter. Of course you don't need our approval, but you *do* need a positive environmental study. Which you don't have."

"No one knows..." Hunter stopped talking and

glanced at me. I pushed through the door and let it close behind me but stayed close to hear the rest of his remarks.

"No one knows about Benny's report. Just bury it," he said quietly.

"Why would we do that?" I heard Crystal ask. "Two people were murdered, and you want us to lie for you? You disgust me, Hunter. All you care about is selling your land for top dollar."

"She's right," Senator Nash said. "Once the murders are solved, we'll move forward with something. Now sit down and enjoy the food. I spent a lot of money for this venue, and I expect everyone to behave and enjoy it."

I heard the sound of a chair scrapping along the floor. "I don't have time to wait for that," Hunter said. "I'm leaving. I need a plan now."

Lily tapped my arm and hissed, "What are you doing here?"

"Listening to them argue and make accusations."

"Crystal, where were *you* when Benny was murdered?" Mick asked. The clink of a cup on a saucer punctuated his question.

Lily moved closer to me as we tilted our heads toward the door so we could hear better.

"*Me*?" she said indignantly.

"Yes, you."

"Working."

"On the senator's boat? Isn't that where you like to spend your mornings?"

I covered my mouth with my hand, so I didn't gasp and reveal our eavesdropping. I looked at Lily, seeing my wide eyes mirrored in hers.

"Come on Mick, lay off. Crystal and I were working on my speech for the ceremony at the new hospital. Then I had appointments for the rest of the morning."

Lily pulled me into the kitchen. "Get back in there with the chowder."

Rose had just finished filling the soup bowls, so I picked up the tray and returned to the dining room.

Just as I entered, I heard Crystal ask, "What about Sunny? She was dead set against the golf course, and she was with Benny on his boat. Have they ruled her out as a suspect?"

Again, starting with Hunter who must have changed his mind about leaving, I set a bowl in front of him.

"Means, motive, and opportunity. What else do the police need?" Crystal asked.

"I'd say she's guilty of something or why else would she keep avoiding you, Mick?" Senator Nash said. "Plus, when I stopped by her house to give her our condolences, her neighbor came out waving a gun in the air. Something is strange with her all right."

"You were at her house?" Mick asked. "Was that before or after it got ransacked."

The senator put his spoon down. "I don't know. Sunny wasn't home and I left."

"And that dog of hers," Crystal said. "It's more like a small car. I wouldn't be surprised if it would kill someone just for fun. Maybe the dog killed Benny."

The senator and Mick chuckled, which made my blood boil.

"That's ridiculous," Hunter said. "Jasper is about as sweet as they come. Sure, she's big, but for your information the big dogs are soft and squishy like a marshmallow. It's those little yippy yappy dogs that you have to watch out for."

Was he talking about Pip? I cleared my throat. I couldn't help it.

"Oh, not *your* adorable little pup." Hunter said to me. "She's a sweetheart. Where is she?"

As if on cue, Pip pushed into the dining room and looked at everyone before she dashed to my side and yipped.

"What is it?" I asked. I didn't miss Crystal's dramatic eye roll. I didn't care if she thought I was nuts to talk to my dog. Anyone with a dog would understand, and obviously, she wasn't a member of that group.

I crouched down to Pip's level and decided to mess with Crystal a bit. "Jasper said what? You're kidding." I scooped Pip into my arms. "Apparently there's some new evidence that has been brought to my attention. I have to find Detective Crenshaw." I said to the group staring at me.

"Your dog told you that?" Crystal asked. "Now I've heard everything."

"Are you going to share it?" Mick asked. "We'd all love a good laugh." A ripple of chuckles circled around the table.

"It's about the murder weapon," I bluffed.

No one laughed now.

I looked around the table as they all—Crystal, Hunter, Mick, and Senator Nash—sent accusing glances at each other.

Which one was the killer?

*a*s I left the dining room in a stunned silence, a plan came together.

"Lily? I said, when back in the kitchen. "Can you and Rose handle the rest of the brunch?" I threw the white shirt I'd borrowed onto a chair.

"What's going on, Dani?" My grandmother gave me her, I-know-you're-up-to-something, piercing stare under raised eyebrows.

I leaned on the island, not sure exactly how to explain my plan. "I just heard that Senator Nash has a boat. I want to find out more about it, especially since Crystal has a habit of hanging out there in the mornings. Since they," I nodded toward the dining room, "are still busy with brunch, this is the time to look for answers."

"Not by yourself you won't," Rose said. "Who's going with you?"

"Maggie?"

"She left with Sunny and Pip. They were both pacing in the office and I couldn't take the nervous energy," Lily said. "They went to Sue Ellen's house to check on Jasper and either stay there or take the dogs for a walk somewhere."

I nodded, digesting that information. "What about Sue Ellen?"

"What about me?" Sue Ellen marched into the kitchen wearing a red apron covered with blue moons. "I'm all set and ready to pitch in."

I smiled at Rose and Lily, seeing my out. "Perfect. Sue Ellen can take over my duties and I'll pop over to talk to Maggie and Sunny."

"I don't like this," Rose said.

"Don't worry. I'll be careful," I said, but of course, danger could be right around any corner. With all the suspects in this case here for the moment, I intended to act quickly and take advantage of this small window of opportunity.

"I'll call Luke," I said as I walked out the door. That would satisfy Rose.

Not wanting to waste a moment, I hurried to Sue Ellen's house. Maggie's sharp voice traveled from the backyard, so I detoured and let myself in through the newly installed gate.

Pip charged and leaped into my arms before Maggie or Sunny even registered my presence.

"Hey, Pipster. Having fun here?"

She answered with a lick of my chin before she squirmed down and dashed off, jumping over Jasper, and racing around her.

"My goodness," Sunny said. "Pip is literally running circles around Jasper. She never gets tired, does she?"

"She settles down when she has to, but this crazy attention means that she really likes Jasper."

"What's up?" Maggie asked. "Why aren't you still helping Lily?" She eyed me suspiciously, letting nothing get past her snooping tendencies.

"Listen, I don't have much time. I found out that Senator Nash has a boat and I want to find out more about it."

"You think *he's* the murderer?" Sunny asked with wide eyes.

"Not necessarily him. I want to ask some questions, find out if he takes the boat out or if someone else does. According to Officer Walker, Crystal spends many mornings on his boat."

"And how would *he* know unless he's there, too?"

Sunny asked showing her disgust with Mick. "That guy is smack in the middle of everyone's business. Makes you wonder, doesn't it?"

"It certainly does, and if I find the senator's boat, maybe I'll find some answers. Want to come along, Mags?"

She fiddled with her phone. "I'd better stay here. Remember that AJ said not to leave Sunny by herself. Unless all three of us go. Would that be too many?"

"Probably. I'll call Luke. He'll come with me."

"Take a look at this, Dani." Maggie held up her phone and Sunny crowded in, too. "This," Maggie said, "is *the Great Escape*, the senator's Boston Whaler. The article says he loves to fish and hunt with his assistant, Ms. Crystal Tilson, in his down time. I'd say that's the boat you're looking for."

"It's not a cigarette boat like you saw leaving Blueberry Bay," Sunny said, disappointment dripping from her comment.

"But it's a boat and it's worth finding out if anyone took it out recently," I said.

Sunny zoomed the photo bigger. She grabbed my arm. "Hey, look who's driving while the senator fishes."

"Crystal! Isn't *she* a multi-talented woman?" I said with too much sarcasm.

"Let me see that." Maggie took her phone back. "Is that a lime green jacket she's wearing? Hideous. Totally not her color."

"I've seen a jacket like that before," Sunny said, carefully studying the photo. "Yeah, on Benny's boat after I found him dead."

I slipped my phone from my pocket to call Luke, not caring one bit about Crystal's fashion sense. Before I pressed his number, the gate clicked, and he walked in. This was no coincidence.

"Rose told me I'd find you here," he said. "She sounded worried."

Of course, she'd called Luke when I left the inn, not trusting me to follow through on my promise. I led him back to the gate as I told him about the senator's boat. "I'm not sure where to start, but I want to find out more about that boat."

"I have an idea," Luke said, opening his truck passenger door for me. "Ace said he'd help if there was anything he could do, and I know he's not busy today. What if he can fly us along the coastline? Wouldn't that be the fastest way to locate the *Great Escape*?"

Another helicopter ride? I froze with one leg

inside the truck, the other firmly planted on the ground like it had suddenly grown roots. Luke gave me a gentle boost to get me moving, not realizing my problem.

Or, maybe he did, because his tender show of encouragement forced me to face my fear.

Head on.

I *could* just say no.

With a determination I didn't know I possessed, I told myself, yes, I would go up in the helicopter again. I'd do it. I had to. I needed to finally push through this irrational fear of heights and free myself of it for once and for all.

I smiled, letting a new strength course through my body. A strength that lifted me beyond my fears.

When Luke had walked around his truck and slipped behind the wheel, he looked at me before starting the engine. "What do you think?"

I loved how he'd given me this perfect opportunity to let *me* figure this out without pushing. I reached across the seat and took his hand. "Call Ace. We don't have any time to waste."

Luke squeezed my hand. With him at my side and Pip too, of course, I'd succeed.

The truck engine purred to life. "I know where to find him." Luke looked at me with a sly grin. He knew exactly what he'd just done and was pleased with the outcome. "Are you ready to do this?"

Did he mean ready to go up in the helicopter again or search for Senator Nash's boat?

It didn't matter because I was ready for both.

I nodded with confidence.

37

*W*hen we arrived at the small airport in Pineville, Ace was in the office focused on his computer.

Luke knocked on the open door. "Got a minute?" he asked.

Ace looked up and grinned. He slammed his laptop closed. "I've got all day. These bills can wait."

Luke nudged me. "Tell Ace the plan."

Did we have an actual plan? "I... we... Senator Nash—"

"What Dani's trying to say," Luke said, "is that Senator Nash has a boat and she'd like to find it. Can you fly us along the coastline? The name of his boat is..." Luke looked at me.

"*Great Escape*," I said. "It's not a cigarette boat like

we saw leaving around the time Benny was murdered, but who knows? Maybe he or someone else took it out and was up to no good."

"And maybe the cigarette boat just caught our attention because of how it was speeding away," Ace said as if this was an angle he should have considered long before now. "What kind of boat does the senator have?"

I pulled up the same article Maggie had found and showed it to Ace and Luke."

Ace whistled showing his admiration. "With a price tag of a half million for that model of Boston Whaler, I'd bet my helicopter that there aren't too many around here. When do you want to go?"

"Now?" I asked.

"We can be in the air in fifteen minutes." Ace walked to the door and held his arm out. "After you."

Without hesitation, I strode toward Ace's helicopter with Pip dashing ahead of me. She knew where we were going and looked excited for another helicopter ride. Maybe she thought she'd be able to catch herself a seagull this way. I chuckled at that thought. She looked at me and yipped. "Is that it, Pipster?" I asked.

"Is what it?" Ace asked me. Apparently, he wasn't used to our style of communication.

"She's hoping to catch a seagull."

"No chance of that. I stay as far away from birds as possible. Hitting one could do a lot of damage or send us into an emergency landing."

He must have seen the color drain from my face.

"Don't worry, Dani. I've never hit a bird, and I don't plan on letting today ruin my perfect flying record." He opened the door and waited for me to step inside. Luke went around and let himself in while Ace made sure my seat belts were properly fastened before I let Pip jump onto my lap.

"We'll head toward Misty Harbor and make a big circle around the whole bay. How does that sound?" He handed me binoculars. "These might help you read the names of the boats."

"What happens if I spot it?"

"Have Luke tap my shoulder, and I'll find a place to land. Unless you'd rather return here so you have your car."

I nodded, deciding I'd figure that out when the time was right. It would all depend on what we saw.

Ace started the engine.

The rotors above us roared to life.

I took a deep breath to settle my nerves and hugged Pip close. Luke smiled at me with his two thumbs up. This adventure filled me with excitement, not fear; determination, not panic. And before I had another second for reflection, the helicopter lifted off the ground, sending us toward the puffy white clouds.

As the houses, trees, and boats on Blueberry Bay shrank away, I relaxed, enjoying this new freedom. Pip, tap dancing on my thighs as she strained to get closer to the window, brought me back to the reason for this trip.

I lifted the binoculars, letting the scene below zoom closer. Everything appeared serene—a beautiful postcard image. Were there clues hidden in this tranquil view?

Pip yipped and scratched at the window. "What is it, Pipster?" I used the binoculars to scan the shoreline.

There, tied fore and aft to buoys in a protected inlet, I spotted a boat that resembled Senator Nash's. I tapped Luke's arm, motioning for him to signal for Ace to circle back and go as low as possible. I had to get a better angle to read the name of the boat.

The helicopter began a turn and descent.

The letters came into focus—*Great Escape*—and a spot of lime green moved along the shore.

Ace glanced back at me.

I made a motion jabbing my thumbs down, hoping he understood that I wanted him to land.

He nodded.

An open field came into view and the helicopter gently settled down. This machine, loud but graceful, was absolutely amazing.

Ace left the helicopter running and yelled over the noise, "I'll wait here."

Luke, Pip, and I jumped out, keeping our heads ducked even though the rotors were well above us. The turbulence whipped my hair into a tangled mess, but Luke grabbed my hand and guided me away from the disturbance.

He pushed my hair behind my ears. "Ace will wait here for us. What are we doing next?"

"I saw someone over there." I pointed toward the water. "Let's see who it is."

Pip took off, headed in the opposite direction.

"You follow her," Luke said. "I'll see if I can find anyone."

I made a beeline toward a thicket of bushes, angry that Pip took this moment to chase chipmunks. Luke disappeared in the direction of the inlet I'd seen. I'd catch up with him after I corralled Pip.

Her stubby tail disappeared on the other side of

a jumble of rose hips. I followed a path around the thicket instead of taking the short route straight through like Pip. The whole time, I scolded myself for not leaving her with Sunny, Maggie, and Jasper instead of losing this precious time.

"Pip!" I yelled. I picked up my pace around the rose hip bushes.

"Oof!"

"Crystal? What are you doing here?" I said, catching her arms and keeping her on her feet after plowing right into her.

"What are *you* doing here?" she asked, obviously unhappy with my presence.

How could I explain why I was out here in the middle of nowhere? "I... the helicopter had to make an emergency landing... we hit a seagull." I stuttered my way through that lie hoping it sounded believable.

"Oh, my goodness! Are you okay? Is anyone with you?"

"I'm fine. Ace stayed with his helicopter. When we got out to check everything, my dog ran off."

Crystal gently took me by my arm. I felt a touch of guilt for lying to her.

"Listen," she said, "my house is just over that knoll. Come in and sit down for a minute. I'll change into my hiking shoes and help you look for your dog."

The little hairs on the back of my neck raised. "Oh, don't worry. I don't want to trouble you. I'll look by myself." I didn't want to risk that her show of kindness might be hiding an ulterior motive to get me out of view.

She shrugged. "Whatever. I was only trying to be helpful."

"Crystal? Before we had to land, I saw a boat. Is it yours?"

Her eyes narrowed and she stepped closer to me. A hint of coffee aroma hit my nose. "Ace Osborn is an excellent pilot. He didn't have to make an emergency landing, did he? Are you snooping around here?"

I stepped away. A rustling in the rose hips caught my attention. "Pip! Come here, girl!" I'd never been so relieved to see my little terrier as I scooped her up and nuzzled my face into her neck.

Feeling emboldened with Pip in my arms, I asked, "It's the senator's boat bobbing offshore, isn't it?"

"Yeah, it is. He lets me use it. Why?"

I was this far in, why not jump the rest of the way? "Benny's murderer arrived by boat."

Crystal's face paled. "You need to leave."

I agreed but had to know more about the lime green jacket draped over her shoulder. "That jacket?"

"Hideous, right?" A shadow of a grin swept across her lips. "Josh got matching ones for us and now?" She hugged the jacket like she'd never let it go.

Interesting, I thought as I turned to leave.

38

"*W*ait!" Crystal grabbed my arm.

A surge of adrenaline shot to my fingertips.

"On second thought," Crystal's fingers dug into my bicep and she leaned close to my ear. "You're not leaving yet. I want to know why you insinuated that someone used the senator's boat to get to Benny and murder him."

Pip let out a deep warning throat rumble.

Where the heck was Luke when I needed him? I jerked my arm free. "Maybe if you tell me where you and the senator were on the morning Benny was murdered, it will clear up that issue."

"The senator plans to moor his boat here until he has his own oceanfront property and that's exactly where it was. That morning, I helped the senator, before I met with Josh," Crystal said. She slipped the jacket on.

"Well, isn't that a convenient alibi. You know, with Josh being dead, you can make up anything and he's not around to corroborate it, is he? What was this so-called meeting about? Maybe... oh I don't know... how to stop Benny's environmental study of the golf course?"

Crystal's eyes teared up and she held her left hand out. A giant diamond ring sparkled on her finger. "Not that it's any business of yours, but we were planning when to make a formal announcement of our engagement. There are a few people that won't take the news very well."

"Hunter Bodane?"

Crystal's eyes widened but she said nothing.

"Dani? Is everything ok here?" Thank goodness. I felt my body relax. Luke was finally here to save me from this awkward conversation. I leaned back, letting his arm circle around me, filling me with a sense of security when I needed it most.

"I found Pip," I said. "We'd better get back to the helicopter before Ace thinks we've found another way home."

As we walked away, I had that uneasy feeling of

Crystal staring at us. "If you're trying to find the killer," she yelled, "look right under your nose. Sunny Shaw is the only person who wanted the golf course project to fail."

"But the rest of you wanted to highjack Benny's potentially negative report," I yelled back.

When we were far enough away, I asked Luke, "Crystal has a point, doesn't she? Do you think Sunny has been lying to us all along? She said Benny told her he hadn't found any reason to recommend stopping the project."

We walked in silence for another minute before Luke spoke. "I don't think Sunny killed her friend. Sure, she's emotional and maybe impulsive, but murder? No, I don't think it's possible."

"You're right. She hid the positive report hoping to stop or, at least, slow down the project from moving forward. What if there was someone else who wanted to stop the golf course? I have an idea, but I need to go back and ask Crystal when that report was delivered and how. We know it's fake, but we have to prove it. Tell Ace I'll be there soon."

"But—"

"I'll be fine, Luke. I've got Pip with me and this will only take a few minutes. If it makes you feel better, tell Ace what's going on and then come back. Also, call AJ and tell him where we are."

"Okay."

Luke jogged toward the helicopter, and I turned back to find Crystal. Something she'd said took on a new meaning, and I didn't have much time to get answers. I had a killer to flush out.

I headed over the knoll in search of Crystal's house. Nestled under tall pine trees I spied a gray weathered Cape Cod style cottage—small and cozy. The front door was ajar, so I poked my head in and called, "Crystal?"

Pip, probably hoping to find a chipmunk to chase, dashed around the side while I stepped inside. An unnatural quiet filled the tidy cottage.

A light tap on the door behind me, made me startle and turn. I hoped Crystal wasn't angry that I'd let myself inside.

"You aren't Crystal." I said at the same time Senator Nash looked at me and uttered the same words.

I glanced at the jacket he carried.

"I found this outside. Crystal must have dropped it."

I found that hard to believe from the way I'd seen

her clutching it. Senator Nash tossed the ugly lime green jacket over the back of the sofa.

Bumping into him wasn't my plan when I'd returned to find Crystal. Where was *she*?

Senator Nash stared at me. Every nerve tingled telling me to run but he blocked the exit.

"You're looking for Crystal?" he asked.

Wasn't that obvious? Here I was standing in her house. "Yeah, but I can come back later. I don't think she's here," I said hoping I sounded believable.

"Too bad about that. Maybe I can help you." He remained in the same spot, giving no indication of moving aside.

"Actually," I searched my brain for something witty to just get me out of this situation. "I wanted to ask Crystal if there was a backup plan for Nine Pine Nursery after the negative report for the golf course. It's kind of odd that Benny mailed that report, but," I waved my hand in the air as if it wasn't any of my business, "what do I know?"

The senator's eyes narrowed. "That's exactly what I'd like to know, too, Ms. Mackenzie. What exactly *do* you know?" He stepped closer to me. "You have your nose stuck in everything... you and Sunny Shaw."

Was he trying to intimidate me? I couldn't have

that. I squared my shoulders and stepped toward Mr. High and Mighty Matt Nash.

Movement through the window caught my attention. A helicopter flew overhead. Where was Ace going? For a split second I panicked, thinking he'd left me here, alone.

Then I saw Luke approaching over the crest of the knoll. He paused as I caught his eye through the open door and gave him a quick shake of my head. For now, I thought it best for him to stay in the background until I got more information about why Senator Nash was looking for Crystal.

"You must be terribly upset about Benny's report giving a thumbs down to your golf course project," I said to the senator.

"*My* project? I never endorsed it. No, that was Crystal's baby. I humored her for the sake of her relationship with Josh Whiting. I don't know *what* she saw in that guy," he added.

As we talked, I inched my way closer to the open door.

"I've been wondering about that report," I said. "How interesting that Benny mailed you something before he was murdered when he still planned to take more photographs of the coastline. Very strange, don't you think? Without it, would the project have just gotten a green light?"

The senator grinned at me. "We'll never know, will we?"

"Unless, there is another report out there."

"What?" his eyes turned dark in a flash. My comment caught him by surprise. He moved and completely blocked the sliver of space I'd planned to sneak through. "Even if Benny gave that friend of his a preliminary report, no one will believe it now."

"Maybe, maybe not," I said. "I'm heading out to find Crystal. I think she knows more about all this than she's shared. She has to be here somewhere."

"I'll go with you," he said, taking my arm.

I didn't like that idea. At all.

Now would be a good time for Luke to swoop in.

Or Pip.

Where were they?

*a*s if Pip heard my thoughts, she rushed to my side, yipping and yapping and making as much commotion as she possibly could.

"What's wrong with that dog?" The senator stamped his foot which seemed to be a silly attempt to scare Pip. Instead, it motivated her.

I crouched down. "Pip? Where's Crystal? Is she in trouble?"

The senator moved in front of me. "You've *got* to be kidding. Are you suggesting that dog understands what you're saying?"

"Of course, she does. And, you know what else?"

"I can't wait to hear this," he said, his voice dripping with sarcasm.

"The dog that was on Benny's boat when he

was murdered?" I paused, watching the senator's jaw muscles clench. "That dog will identify the killer."

"You're crazy."

I focused on Pip. "Maybe, but I'm following my dog to see what she's found. Maybe it's Crystal."

He followed me. We stopped in front of Crystal's house. "Mr. Senator, I'm wondering. Have you made an offer to Hunter Bodane for his waterfront property yet?"

"What?" He seemed perplexed by my question, but his eye twitch gave him away.

I kept digging. "Yeah, Crystal told me that you want waterfront property so you'll have your *own* dock for your boat. When she told me that, it got me to thinking. I said to myself, a man like Senator Nash would insist on regular updates from someone he hired to do an important study. So... when Benny told he'd give the project a green light, you lost it. You had to stop him before that study was released. You wanted Hunter in a corner so you could buy that property for yourself. Right, Mr. Senator?" I leaned right in his face. "And you killed Josh too, when he figured it out. Right?"

"Are you listening to what you're saying? It's nonsense. Who will believe you?"

"I think the question is: who will believe *you*, Mr. Senator."

We stared at each other.

My heart raced.

He flinched.

I was ready when he lunged toward me, and I easily jumped to the side, stumbling over some shrubbery.

My move made the senator lose his balance. Pip dashed over, barking to alert anyone nearby, and circled around Senator Nash, giving Luke time to reach me.

AJ's SUV screeched to a halt. Officer Walker was out before AJ even had time to open his door.

Maggie, Sunny, Ace, and Jasper ran over the knoll toward us. As they got closer, Jasper zeroed in on Senator Nash.

"Where's Crystal?" I stood over the senator who cowered in a fetal position. "Tell me or I'll let Jasper tear you limb-from-limb." To prove my point, I held her collar and let her come within inches of him.

He squirmed away but we followed.

Jasper slobbered on him.

"She's in her bedroom." He frantically rolled away from Jasper, protecting his head with his arms.

"You're pathetic. You know where you made a

mistake, Mr. Senator? You left Josh's jacket on Benny's boat. Crystal and Josh were together, planning their engagement announcement when he was murdered, so your sleazy plan to frame Josh backfired. You wanted that land, so badly, you even fabricated a phony report." I shook my head, filled with rage at this person who'd assumed he could get away with anything. "It was so easy for you to turn one murder into two. Who'd you plan to kill next —Crystal?"

Luke pulled me away, shushing me as he stroked my hair. "It's over now, Dani. AJ and Officer Walker have everything under control." I let him lead me away. I'd said what needed saying.

Maggie led Crystal out. "He had her gagged and tied up on the floor of her closet. Dani, if you hadn't come back—"

Crystal broke away from Maggie and flung her arms around me. "He was going to kill me, but he heard you call my name. I thought he'd kill us both." She buried her face on my shoulder and sobbed. "Thank you. The senator had me convinced that Sunny was the murderer. I was a blind fool about his shenanigans."

After a flurry of activity, Senator Nash was driven off to the police station, Crystal left in an ambulance, and the rest of us—Luke, Maggie, Sunny, and me, plus the two dogs—followed Ace to his helicopter.

"What made you think to bring Maggie, Sunny, and Jasper?" I asked as we walked.

"Well," he said with a grin, "I didn't like it that you went back, but Luke here, said you had to do what you had to do. And, I guess that's how I operate, too. I wanted reinforcements just in case, so Luke told me to call your friend, Maggie." Ace glanced at her with a look that would make most women's toes curl. I wasn't sure if she noticed.

"Anyway," he continued, "she told us where I could pick them up, and I'm glad I followed my gut." Ace slapped me on my back. "Now, Luke has a surprise for you so you can put this all behind you. Are you ready?"

"Does it involve your helicopter?"

"It sure does. Hop in."

I did and I enjoyed every moment of the flight, with Pip on my lap. The view below was the best—Blueberry Bay shimmering under the afternoon sun, with splashes of color from the boats below. It didn't matter where he took us because we'd left our problems behind.

Like magic, Ace set his helicopter on the ground as gently as a hummingbird landing on a flower.

"I made some last-minute plans," Luke said as I looked around and tried to figure out where we were. "It's not exactly the picnic I'd originally planned but sometimes improvising is the name of the game."

He took my hand.

With Jasper and Pip in the lead, we slowly walked to a point of land that jutted over Blueberry Bay.

"Beautiful, isn't it?" Sunny asked. "Hunter told me that Crystal called him after she bumped into you and you asked about the senator's boat. She realized that he'd never been too excited about the golf course and had let slip that a piece of waterfront land would be coming his way soon. She was so alarmed that she called Hunter and asked him if the senator had made an offer."

"Had he?"

Sunny nodded. "Crystal convinced Hunter to contact the conservation group right away, and he called me with his decision to sell the land to them just before we all got to Crystal's cottage."

That filled in a few details for me.

"How'd you figure it out? And why on earth did you confront the senator?" Sunny asked.

"It was that lime green jacket plus the senator

needing property for his boat. I didn't plan to confront him. I wanted to ask Crystal more questions, but when I got back, he ambushed me." I looked out over the bay. "What a relief that this land will be kept in its natural state forever."

"I'm going to do everything I can to get them to name it after Benny." A tear slid down Sunny's cheek. "I think he'd appreciate that."

"Ready for that picnic we had planned?" Luke asked.

I looked around. "Where?"

"Come on." He took my hand again and we followed a path to a spot surrounded by boulders and rose hips. "Close your eyes, Dani."

"Seriously? I'll trip."

"I'll take care of that." In one quick swoop, Luke cradled me in his arms. "No peeking," he whispered.

"Eek!" He'd surprised me but I quickly settled into the nest of his arms, inhaling his salty, piney scent.

After a bumpy couple of minutes, he gently set me on my feet. "Okay. Open your eyes."

For the second time that day, the magic of the moment overwhelmed me. Blankets covered the ground showcasing all my favorite foods. Lily walked over with two glasses of wine for Luke and me. "You've earned this, Dani."

"How—"

"Luke's been planning this surprise for days. Be thankful you're here. We were afraid you'd miss your own special picnic. Now... relax and enjoy yourself," Lily said.

Luke clinked his glass against mine. "To the best six months of my life."

"I'll drink to that," I said, leaning against the love of my life and wallowing in the warm happiness filling me.

MORE BLUEBERRY BAY

Welcome to Blueberry Bay, a scenic region of Maine peppered with quaint small towns and home to a shocking number of mysteries. If you loved this book, then make sure to check out its sister series from other talented Cozy Mystery authors...

Pet Whisperer P.I.
By Molly Fitz

Glendale is home to Blueberry Bay's first ever talking cat detective. Along with his ragtag gang of human and animal helpers, Octo-Cat is determined to save the day... so long as it doesn't interfere with his schedule. Start with book one, *Kitty Confidential*, which is now available to buy or borrow! Visit Visit www.QuirkyCozy.com/PetWhisperer for more.

⚔️

Little Dog Diner
By Emmie Lyn

Misty Harbor boasts the best lobster rolls in all of Blueberry Bay. There's another thing that's always on the menu, too. Murder! Dani and her little terrier, Pip, have a knack for being in the wrong place at the wrong time... which often lands them smack in the middle of a fresh, new murder mystery and in the crosshairs of one cunning criminal after the next. Start with book one, *Mixing Up Murder*, which is now available to buy or borrow! Visit www.QuirkyCozy.com/LittleDog for more.

⚔️

Shelf Indulgence
By S.E. Babin

Dewdrop Springs is home to Tattered Pages, a

popular bookshop specializing in rare editions, a grumpy Persian cat named Poppy, and some of the most suspicious characters you'll ever meet. And poor Dakota Adair has just inherited it all. She'll need to make peace with her new cat and use all her book smarts to catch a killer or she might be the next to wind up dead in the stacks. Start with book one, *Hardback Homicide*, which is now available to buy or borrow! Visit www.QuirkyCozy.com/Shelf-Indulgence for more.

🍴

Haunted Housekeeping
By R.A. Muth

Cooper's Cove is home to Blueberry Bay's premier estate cleaning service. Tori and Hazel, the ill-fated proprietors of Bubbles and Troubles, are prepared to uncover a few skeletons. But when a real one turns up, they'll have to solve the mystery quickly if they're going to save their reputations—and their lives. Book one, *The Squeaky Clean Skeleton,* will be coming soon. Keep an eye on www.QuirkyCozy.com/HauntedHousekeeping for more.

♈

The Cursed Cat of Caraway
By F.M. Storm

Quiet, secluded, and most importantly, far away from his annoying magical family, Guy couldn't wait to start a new life on Caraway Island. Unfortunately, he hadn't counted on his four-year-old daughter coming into her own witchy powers early... or on her accidentally murdering one of the PTO moms. Oops! Book one, *The Kindergarten Coven*, will be coming soon. Keep an eye on www.QuirkyCozy.com/CursedCat for more.

MORE EMMIE!

I hope you enjoyed this book.

Click here to sign up for my newsletter and never miss a new release.

🍴

About Emmie Lyn

Emmie Lyn shares her world with her husband, a rescue terrier named Underdog, and a black cat named Ziggy. When she's not busy thinking of ways to kill off a character, she loves enjoying tea and chocolate in her flower garden, hiking, or spending time near the ocean.

Emmielynbooks.com

🍴

More Emmie!

Cozy Mysteries

Little Dog Diner Cozy Mystery Series

Mixing Up Murder

Serving Up Suspects

Dishing Up Deceit

Cooking Up Chaos

Crumbling Up Crooks

Dicing Up Disaster

🍴

COMING SOON ...

New cozy mystery series:

Mint Chocolate Chip Mysteries

🍴

Romantic Suspense:

Gold Coast Retriever Series

Helping Hanna

Shielding Shelly

71759352R00177